DROW MYSTERY

DROW MYSTERY

CHRONICLES OF SHADOW BOURNE™ BOOK 3

MARTHA CARR

MICHAEL ANDERLE

DISRUPTIVE IMAGINATION™

LMBPN Publishing
2375 E. Tropicana Avenue, Suite 8-305
Las Vegas, Nevada 89119 USA

Version 1.00, January 2024
ebook ISBN: 979-8-88878-254-5
Print ISBN: 979-8-88878-787-8

THE DROW MYSTERY TEAM

Thanks to our JIT Readers

Dorothy Lloyd
Diane L. Smith
Jeff Goode
Christopher Gilliard

Editor

SkyFyre Editing Team

CHAPTER ONE

Ellis locked the bathroom door, leaned against the sink, and waited for the automatic overhead lighting to click off. The familiar darkness should have been comforting, but anxiety crackled up her arms.

Ellis hadn't been able to use her shadow magic in over a month. The pools of umber and violet in the room's corners mocked her. She glared at them, then plunged her fingers into the darkness.

Nothing.

"Mother Below," Ellis whispered. It was half-curse and half-prayer. The Mother Below was the patron goddess of caves and shadows, and Ellis had apparently risen out of her grace into the light.

She grumbled and waved her arms until the motion-activated lights flickered back on.

Without shadow magic, it would be much harder to sneak into Amelia's office. Even after 8:00 pm on a Wednesday, Amelia would still be there.

Ellis removed her grandmother's moonsteel lockpicks

from her bun. She stroked the opalescent metal and remembered the birthday on which she'd received them.

Nan Elandra had lived to the formidable age of two hundred and six, impossible for a human and ancient for a drow. She'd died when Ellis was eight, which was the year Ellis' life had veered from hard to unbearable.

The Industrial Revolution had pushed the drow away from the human world, and the advent of modern technology had sent them underground for good. Ellis' grandmother remembered the time before a hundred feet of sedimentary rock separated the two races.

Back then, the border between the real and the unreal had been fuzzier. There was room for myths to intrude on history and the magical and physical to interact. Ellis was not the first human Nan Elandra had met.

Nan Elandra had robbed some of those humans blind.

Whenever Ellis had a difficult time in the crèche, she'd go to her grandmother's small, dim chambers, and Nan Elandra would hook her cane around the handle of a wicker basket under her bed and pull out a treasure trove of locks. Some were old, nineteenth-century Polhem padlocks and mortice locks from the Roaring Twenties, but some were new. One had been stamped with a recent year. Ellis had never asked where her grandmother had obtained it.

Ellis' grandmother would then pull the moonsteel pins out of her silver hair, which fell over her shoulders like water in moonlight. Her hands cramped too badly to pick the locks herself, but she instructed Ellis on how to hold the pressure with the first pick while she worked the tumblers with the second. When Ellis made a mistake, Nan would pound her cane on the floor, which rattled the locks in the basket. Ellis would shriek, and they would laugh.

Nan also taught her to pick pockets. Nan's eyes would crinkle as she circled her cane like a maypole while Ellis attempted to steal mushroom sweets. She'd say, "A time will come when the drow must leave their hidey holes. When that day arrives, they'd best have a few who can survive on the Upside."

Ellis had learned fast.

She considered her reflection. The grass-green romper she'd bought from a Highland Park boutique now struck her as idiotically flashy. She was accustomed to disappearing, so dressing conspicuously did not come naturally, but it was too late to change.

She left the bathroom and hugged the shadows along the wall in the corridor that led to Amelia's office. The thick hardwood door bore an elegant brass plaque with Amelia's name inside an embossed border of bromeliads.

Ellis rapped her knuckles below the plaque. When there was no response, she pressed her ear to the door. The only noise was the low hum of the air conditioning blowing through the leaves of potted plants.

Ellis tried the handle, which rattled without turning. She slipped the lockpicks into the keyhole.

Hector called her name from down the hallway.

Ellis instinctively reached for the shadows inside the keyhole to shroud herself, but it was as useless as pushing the wrong ends of two magnets together. The hot resistance seared her fingertips, and when Ellis yanked her hand back, she left the moonsteel lockpick behind.

Ellis spun toward the Bromeliad's jack-of-all-trades

facilities manager, carefully blocking his view of the lock-pick stuck in the door. Tight chocolate-brown corduroys hugged his muscular legs, and his smile pushed Ellis' anxiety into fluttery, unfamiliar terrain.

"Amelia's gone," Hector informed her. "She went to a fundraiser at the Natural History Museum."

"That's a shame. I meant to drop something off before I left."

"I can give it to her tomorrow morning. I have to be here at oh-dark-thirty to meet the wholesaler for the café."

"That's okay. Don't worry about it."

Hector's mica-gray eyes sparkled as he held out a calloused hand. "Please. I know how Amelia is about her deliverables."

Ellis smiled wanly, cursed silently, and reached into her bag. *You could have just said you needed to talk to her.*

Her fingers closed around a cool metal object attached to a wide titanium ring—the prototype grapnel Percy had helped her make. He'd designed internal electronics to replace some of the bulky mechanical controls so she could ditch the clunky utility belt.

She couldn't give Hector the grapnel, but his suspicion was growing. The next item she grabbed was a blackout silk bag, and she hauled the frictionless fabric out of her purse and thrust it into Hector's hands.

"Here!" she blurted, then pasted on a too-bright smile. "Thanks so much!"

He frowned at the midnight-black material. "What *is* this?"

Young drow used blackout silk bags to develop their shadow magic skills. The fabric was so tightly woven that it admitted no light, so the darkness within was a potent source of magic. Ellis had taken to carrying one in the hope that the educational tool would provide a whisper of her old powers. It hadn't.

"Um, it's a sleep mask," Ellis ventured.

Hector lit up. "How does it work? The light from the building beside mine shines into my bedroom window, and my blackout curtains aren't cutting it."

"I'll show you." She snatched the silk back, then eased the material over her head and tightened the drawstring. Rich, deep darkness enveloped her. A year ago, it would have been comforting.

She stuck out her arms in a magician's *ta-da*. "See?"

Hector snorted. "You look like you're about to be guillotined, but okay."

He pulled the bag off her head, and she winced at the brightness in the hall. Then, she stifled giggles as he put the bag on and murmured appreciatively. It *did* look funny.

Hector removed it and held it up to the light. "What's it made of?"

Ellis froze. "Uh, special silk…made in Italy…by nuns. Blind nuns."

Hector blinked, then shrugged. "Cool."

Dammit, Ellis! Too many details. Nan Elandra had never dealt with humans who'd learned to Google before they'd learned to walk.

Hector waved the bag cheerfully. "Anyway, thanks for the tip. I'll ensure that Amelia gets it."

Ellis bit her lip. That was her only blackout silk bag. She couldn't stroll into the Homestead to get another one.

Hector stuffed the bag into his pocket. "While you're

here, I know it's late, but could you take a look at a mushroom problem?"

Sadly, it was not a euphemism. Ellis acquiesced, and after Hector turned around, she hurriedly popped the lockpick out of the lock before she followed him to the elevator. On the way, they chatted about the newest season of *Sven on the Ice*, in which Sven was betrayed by Hilde, his long-term partner.

The Norwegian crime drama was the only TV show Ellis had watched in its entirety. Her limited pop culture knowledge made talking about popular media dangerous territory. Questions like, "What's a mermaid?" tended to raise eyebrows, so it was a relief to meet a superfan of the one series with which she was deeply familiar.

In the elevator, Hector selected sub-basement two, which housed their mushroom grow-op. Ellis stared at the keyhole beside the button for sub-basement three. The secret level taunted her, but a camera hung from the ceiling. Picking the lock was the first item on her "when my shadow magic comes back" list.

If it comes back.

"How long have you been working for Amelia?" Ellis kept her tone light. Hector was an excellent coworker but a brick wall when it came to personal questions.

"Long enough," he replied amiably.

"How much do you know about her?"

"Why?" The amiability transmuted into questioning.

Ellis plastered a stupid smile on her face. That usually deflected suspicion. "She's impressive. Definitely a role model."

Hector's broad shoulders relaxed. "I certainly wouldn't want to be her enemy."

That was an interesting response. Was it an innocent comment or a threat? Ellis decided not to push her luck.

The digital display ticked down to sub-basement two, and the door opened onto a warren of narrow corridors and locked doors with a *ding*.

Ellis often worked on the mushroom grow-op, and she'd never run into anyone but Hector, so she'd already picked many of the locks. So far, she'd only found dusty junk like stacks of old office furniture, discontinued hotel linens, and obsolete computers. The closest thing to danger she'd encountered was boxes of old invoices that threatened to bore her to death.

She found it a pleasant place to work. It had been weeks before she'd realized that it reminded her of the Swallow's Nest and she missed the homestead more than she wanted to admit. Moving surface-side had highlighted her drow heritage in ways she'd never dreamed of.

Hector opened a silver door at the end of the corridor. The gentle hiss told Ellis that the climate control systems were working. The light inside was lovely and dim, with a faint pink glow from the heartstopper mushrooms.

Harsh light flooded the room when Hector flicked a switch. Ellis resisted the urge to grumble. It wasn't his fault he couldn't see in the dark.

The grow-op occupied four rooms in the sub-basement: one each for storage, inoculation, incubation, and fruiting. Comfortingly familiar sawdust filled the storage room, but the rest of the equipment was more scientific than Ellis was used to. That had turned out to be a boon when her shadow magic gave out.

The fruiting room, where the mushrooms grew to full size, had the square footage of a small apartment and spotless concrete floors. Floor-to-ceiling metal racks lined the walls, and there were two freestanding racks in the middle. A blocky air conditioning unit sat at the back. It was supposed to be a perfect all-in-one climate maintenance solution.

"What's the problem?" Ellis asked.

Hector made a face. "The humidity. The unit isn't providing any moisture."

Ellis stood in the middle of the room and drew a deep breath of cool air. The temperature felt right, but it *was* arid. "Fourteen percent?" she estimated.

The wall-mounted digital monitor showed that she was spot on. "How do you *do* that?"

"Practice." The real answer was, she had a drow father who was a stickler for tradition. The drow could acquire modern humidity meters, but Connor Burton preferred to control his environments by feel and instinct.

Ellis grabbed a small screwdriver from the workbench and opened the enormous AC unit's case. The evaporators were working, and none of the lines were clogged. She checked everything from the intake to the outlet but found no problems.

After she closed the case, Ellis put her hand over the outlet and felt moist, almost misty air. *Curious.* She paced the room with her hands outstretched. Near the door, the air was desert-dry. Was something wrong with the growth medium?

She admired the vibrant rustcaps in a nearby tray, then plucked one. Its dusty, ferrous coating rubbed off on her fingers as she popped the mushroom into her mouth. It was like eating a soft penny. The café wouldn't be rushing to do a rustcap stroganoff any time soon.

When Ellis swallowed, a rush of energy drove her pulse against the small capillaries in her temples.

Watching the change in her face, Hector chuckled. "They *are* remarkable, aren't they?"

Ellis nodded, then considered the heartstoppers. They were smaller than a thumbnail, and their bright pink spots were so vivid that she'd had to convince Hector they weren't poisonous. In the Swallow's Nest, people grew them for their beautiful pink glow as much as their aphrodisiac properties.

She wasn't sure it would be wise to binge aphrodisiacs in an enclosed space with a coworker, even if he *did* look nice in that soft cotton shirt.

She wandered over to the midnight blues instead. She'd never had much use for the dark, feathery cones, which improved skin moisture and elasticity. Maybe she would change her mind when she was Amelia's age. Extra skin moisture would be welcome in this dry air, however.

The specimen she pulled out looked fine. "Down the hatch." She broke the fleshy trumpet in two and offered the other half to Hector. He took it and grimaced when he put it in his mouth.

Ellis picked a speck on the wall to focus on as she chewed. Her grandmother said midnight blues tasted like month-old meat from a cave goat with a bad personality, and her grandmother had *liked* midnight blues.

Ellis suppressed a gag as the rotten flavor spread over her tongue. "Ugh. They taste like they're supposed to."

Hector shuddered, then sympathetically offered her a bottle of water, which she gratefully swigged. "*Nothing* should taste like that."

Ellis frowned. Everything looked and tasted right, so why were her lips chapping? "Have you noticed anything?"

"The midnight blues are going through woodchips at twice the rate they're supposed to. Don't know if that means anything."

Ellis peered into the plastic-wrapped blocks of wood-chips. The mushrooms looked fine, but the growth matrix had sunk, as though the underlying structure had caved in.

Ellis poked the hole left by the midnight blue she'd picked, and something wiggled under her finger. She yelped and pulled it out.

"What's wrong?" Hector's skin was a shade paler. Instead of meeting her gaze, he looked at a spot just above her head, where the overhead light cast flickering shadows. His pupils were black holes that sucked out the color in his irises.

Uh-oh. The trumpet-shaped midnight blues twisted and pressed together like gaping, oxygen-starved lips. Ellis plunged her hand into the growth matrix as her heartbeat sped up. The wood chips pulsed in her hands, and she ignored her brain's insistence that a sleek, limbless predator lurked in the spaces between them.

Her fingers found a hard, round lump. "Oh, shit. I found the problem."

"What is it?"

She held out her hand. The lump was not much to look

at, the size of a raisin and the color of bone china. Ellis had encountered one once before, in her early teens. "It's a nightmare node."

"A *what?*"

Ellis examined the lump, which appeared to pulse. "A nightmare node. It's a parasitic fungus. I've seen it before. Don't freak out. We're hallucinating."

She glanced up and screamed when the metal racks behind Hector buckled in and enfolded him in gnashing silver jaws. Hector shouted in response to her outburst. *So much for don't freak out, Ellis.* She clamped her eyes shut.

When she opened them, the racks were a rectilinear grid, and aside from the extra eyeball on his forehead, Hector was fine.

"It's a parasitic fungus," Ellis repeated. "That's why the humidity has been wonky. They're serious hydrophiles. They've been sucking water from the air."

Hector's face twisted in disbelief. At first, Ellis thought he doubted her diagnosis, but then he yelled, *"How am I supposed to trust a woman with snake hands?"* and backed into the metal racks in the center of the room.

The midnight blues wobbled and released silver powder into the air, which settled on Hector's hair and skin. He started to hyperventilate, and the overhead lights made the tiny hallucinogenic flecks glitter as he sucked them in.

Ellis reached to pull him away from the shelf, but he screamed. *Oh, right. Snake hands. Dammit.* She hid her hands behind her and took a step back. "We have to leave."

Hector vehemently nodded, which shook mushroom dust out of his hair. Ellis kept her hands behind her back and shouldered him to the doorway. In doing so, she received a face-full of spores, and the scent of rotted meat coated her nostrils.

Hector moaned as he approached the door. To Ellis, it stretched to twice its normal height. There was no telling what Hector saw. He shrank back, then steeled himself and opened it with a shaking hand.

A crimson sheen bathed the hall beyond. It resembled slick intestines.

It's not real. Ellis shoved Hector into the hallway, then slammed the door behind them. Snake hands be damned, she pulled him toward the elevator.

"Sunlight!" she exclaimed.

"What?" Hector stopped abruptly, and Ellis slammed into him.

She growled and hit the call button. "That's how we fight it. Sunlight will burn away the hallucinations."

The elevator door opened. Ellis thought she saw something inside leap onto the ceiling.

It's not real, she repeated. She dug her fingernails into Hector's arm and pulled, but he wouldn't budge. He stared into the elevator in terror.

"Come *on!*" she insisted. If they didn't expose themselves to full sunlight within the next twelve hours, the psychic damage could be permanent.

Ellis didn't want to break down any doors. She wrapped her arms around Hector's waist and bent her knees.

Hector yelped in surprise as Ellis threw him over her shoulder and dashed into the elevator. She pressed the button for the top floor with her knee.

He thrashed and pounded her back with closed fists, then went still. When the elevator creaked into motion, she set him on the floor. He crawled into the corner.

"Witch," he whispered. She thought that was what he'd said.

Halfway through rolling her eyes, an unseen pressure pinned them in place. *Oh, Mother! They'll stick like that.* Something was controlling her.

No one's controlling you! You've been poisoned!

Ellis blinked twice. Then she could look at Hector again. "We'll be fine."

He did his best to melt into the floor, and she sighed and moved as far away as she could. Ellis tried not to stare at an undulating shape in the overhead light.

The elevator doors scraped open on the top floor to reveal blackness. Ellis knew there was a normal hallway there, and she forced herself to step into the void.

Ellis manhandled Hector down the hall and up the fire escape stairs, although she didn't have to carry him again. That was good since she wasn't sure how to grip someone with so many tentacles.

One door stood between them and the open air on the rooftop. Then, the helicopter haze of Los Angeles pressed against them like rotors whirring on an enormous eye. The eastern horizon was dark.

Right. It's nighttime.

Maybe the fresh air would help.

Hector scrambled away from some unseen horror toward the edge of the roof, and Ellis grabbed the waistband of his corduroys. No one would dive into traffic on her watch.

"It'll be okay. We just have to make it to dawn," she told him. Hector nodded, then squeezed his eyes shut.

A harpy howled, and Ellis looked up to see a huge, predatory bird. Its talons were poised, its beak was wet, and...its eyes were wrong. One was an evil black bead deep within its turkey-vulture-bald head, and the other was a yolky bulb.

Ellis covered her face with her hands until the horrible vision resolved into comprehensible reality. "*Wormy?*"

Hector's nails dug into her arm. "Don't talk to it!"

"That pigeon is a friend of mine" would raise questions, so Ellis explained, "It's a pigeon. I've fed it Cheetos."

Wormy squawked. In their hallucinogenic haze, it was a world-conquering shriek. Ellis and Hector pressed together and tried to sink into the roof. When she looked up again, Wormy had retreated to the far end of the building.

Dawn came painfully slowly, but eventually, sunlight filtered through the haze. Ellis and Hector crossed to the east side of the building and stretched toward the light on tiptoe. Wormy hopped along the edge of the roof and stared until they took a half-step back.

The dawn light was gentle, but it burned Ellis' skin. The low fire reminded her of eating cinnamon candy, but it pushed back the torrent of hallucinations. Wormy shrank from a looming terror-bird to her true form: an ugly-as-compost pigeon. When she cooed, the noise was pleasant.

Hector, who was regaining his color, suspiciously stared at the pigeon. "There's something wrong with that bird."

Wormy squawked in offense and gyred skyward. Ellis

hoped the pigeon would forgive her or at least not get her in trouble with Percy. *I'd better stock up on Cheetos.*

Hector spread himself out like a cat in the sunlight. When Ellis walked over to him, he complained, "You're in my light," but his face crinkled in a smile.

"I'm so sorry, Hector." She couldn't believe she'd missed the nightmare nodes. They were a rare occurrence in the drow's mushroom caverns. She hadn't anticipated that they could pop up in the human world. *Stupid, Ellis. Underground is underground.* The nodes were probably rare because the mushroom attendants paid attention and prevented them.

Hector nudged her out of the sunlight with a toe. "It's not your fault. Unless... You weren't growing those things intentionally, were you?"

"No. It's a disease. I would have stopped it if I'd noticed."

Hector's eyes reflected the hazy white sky. "That was like being in a horror movie."

"I'm sorry," Ellis insisted.

"Don't be. I love horror movies."

Ellis offered him her hand. He grabbed it, and she easily pulled him to his feet.

A strange look came over his face. "I seem to remember you throwing me over your shoulder like a feather boa."

Ellis loosened her grip. She trusted Hector, or wanted to. He was a competent, reliable, and hardworking mushroom farmer, but he was loyal to Amelia. He dodged every question about the Bromeliad's glamorous owner, who had her finger on anything in LA that had a pulse and some things that didn't.

Until Ellis understood those relationships, she would

be wary of sharing her drow upbringing, and she would not reveal her shadow magic to Hector.

If it ever comes back.

Ellis smiled. "Hallucinations are funny that way. Are you afraid of strong women?"

A faint blush crept up his neck. "Not particularly."

He was too bogged down in Freudian self-reflection to ask questions on the elevator ride back down. The soft *ding* of the doors opening broke the silence.

Framed by the steel doors, Amelia Bronson perched on elegant sky-high stilettos. She took in their tousled, sweaty appearance and raised an amused eyebrow over a knowing smile.

Ellis started. "Why are you here so early?" It was barely 6:00 am.

"Sleep is not the most valuable use of my time," Amelia replied. "Nor yours, it would seem."

Ellis was about to protest when Hector stepped forward with a self-satisfied smile. "Ellis and I were on the roof watching the sunrise."

Amelia wouldn't care if they were sleeping together. She *might* care that a hallucinogenic parasite had contaminated her grow-op.

Amelia tittered delicately and insincerely. "Get some sleep. I need to talk to you about a café project, but it's not urgent." She had a tinge of annoyance in her voice.

"Sure thing, boss."

Amelia disappeared into the elevator with a dismissive wave.

Ellis turned on Hector. "Why did you say..." *That we*

16

were doing the horizontal lambada on the roof? "that we were together on the roof?"

"I didn't say it. I *implied* it," Hector replied. "Don't look so offended. I'm not sure I can take any more psychic wounds tonight."

"She'll think we're totally unprofessional."

"We just poisoned ourselves with the nightmare dust infesting our farm. We *are* unprofessional."

He had a point. Ellis blushed, and she didn't try to hide it. She pictured the flinty look on her father's face if he found out she had let a nightmare node infestation get out of control. He was proud of her fungiculture. Aside from shadow magic, it was the one skill that had given her value in drow society. Now she was a failure as a mushroom farmer *and* as a shadow magician.

Tears welled in Ellis' eyes. She instinctively reached for shadows to conceal her humiliation and came up empty, which made her cry harder.

Hector's eyes widened. "Ellis? Ellis, I'm sorry. I didn't realize it would upset you. I thought it was our best chance of avoiding the third degree. I've only seen Amelia's temper twice, and I do *not* want a Round Three."

Ellis shook her head and wiped her face with her sleeve. "It's fine. It's been a long night. I'll see you later."

She fled to the Bromeliad's garage.

CHAPTER TWO

The drow had a saying: "*Fire wasps attract cave widows.*"

Fire wasps were annoying since they resisted shadow magic, but extermination required only moderate effort. A bad infestation, however, attracted insectivores, particularly cave widows. Cave widow bites would kill you if an antivenin poultice wasn't immediately applied. Therefore, "*Fire wasps attract cave widows*" meant that small problems led to big problems. Percy said the comparable American saying was, "A stitch in time saves nine."

Both sayings came to mind when Ellis' motorcycle broke down on the ride home.

She managed to steer to the shoulder without falling off as the engine sputtered. She dismounted and kicked the tires. The apple-red bike was sleek, small, quiet, and thoroughly unreliable. It had broken down six times since she'd lost Granny, her Harley.

Granny was languishing in the LAPD's impound lot, an unwilling guest of the state. Memories of the old girl chewed at Ellis' guts as she walked the junky red motorcycle along the road. She wanted to take the plates off the bike, dump it in the nearest alley, and let nature take its course. Perhaps everything that was happening to her was a punishment for abandoning Granny.

She couldn't ask Charlie for help. He'd been quiet since the attack at his captain's house. If she was in mortal danger, he'd probably show up, but "I lost my motorcycle during a bank robbery. Help me steal it from your employer" was unlikely to elicit sympathy.

She was exhausted, and hunching over the broken bike made her shoulder ache. She grew more annoyed as she walked, and a rough outline of a plan bloomed.

I might not have shadow magic or mushroom skills, but I'm still a kickass vigilante. Kickass vigilantes don't abandon their noble steeds.

Ellis burst into her apartment. "Who wants to help me rob the LAPD?"

Twelve pairs of eyes blinked at her, one of which was human.

Percy Rawlings, wearing an embroidered silk robe and neon-pink pajama pants, perched on a stool at Ellis' breakfast bar. Complex code covered his laptop screen. Ellis could barely use a cell phone, so she doubted she would ever understand Percy's work.

She blinked at his robe. It appeared to have a fur collar, but Percy was a committed vegan. She realized the luxurious fur was a living animal. Muffler the ferret was wrapped around the pet psychic's neck.

"Ellis! Wormy tells me you had quite the evening. 'Goings-on,' she said."

Ellis glared at her balcony, where Wormy perched on the railing. The pigeon primly stepped behind an aloe plant.

"Wormy ratted me out?" An insulted squeak emanated from within the kitchen, and Ellis tried not to think about her pantry. "Er, *birded* me out? Hector and I had mushroom trouble."

Percy's eyebrows shot up so quickly that they startled the parakeet on his head. "'Hector,' eh?"

"Yes, *Hector.*" Ellis' heart skipped a beat at the memory of his weight on her shoulder.

Percy's expression implied many assumptions.

Ellis huffed. "Don't give me that look."

"What look?" Percy's lashes fluttered over his gray irises.

"Your eyes are twinkling with all the subtlety of police sirens."

"You've spent a lot of time with *Hector,* and Charlie's name hasn't come up recently."

"Yeah, well, the police and I have parted ways."

"You just said you wanted to rob them."

Ellis wrinkled her nose. "I want Granny. That piece of red garbage I bought to replace her broke down again. Hence, who wants to help me rob the LAPD? It can be my parting gift!"

A chorus of squeaks, caws, yowls, and woofs answered her. Even Wormy stepped back out from behind the aloe plant.

"Even if I said no, I'd be outvoted," Percy observed.

"That's the spirit!"

The idea took on a life of its own. *See how* you *like it when Granny disappears from lockup, eh, Charlie?* Ellis imagined his face at the announcement in the bullpen and his anger when he came to confront her.

It was a fantasy. She doubted that problems at the impound lot made it back to the homicide unit. Regardless, his imaginary fury haunted her as the plan developed.

Fortunately, the lot's security cameras were connected to a central system, which Percy could hack. He also found recent satellite images for scoping out escape routes.

He doodled on a piece of printer paper while Ellis examined the images. "Not complicated. Just an electronic chain-link gate. The main problem will be stopping the guards from calling hell down on your sweet head as you ride away."

"I'm not *useless.* Just...underpowered." *More like* un*powered.*

Percy, who was normally a human windup toy, was still and solemn. "Is that what you're on about with this rob-the-police madness? I know you're frustrated, but you've got nothing to prove to me."

She scowled. "What? *No!* This isn't about you. Or my skills. Or Charlie."

"Whoa! Who said anything about Charlie? Your subconscious is outrunning you, girlie."

Ellis glared. "This isn't about anyone but Granny."

"Last I checked, Granny was a non-sentient hunk of metal."

"A non-sentient hunk of sleek American-made metal

with a Milwaukee-8 114 engine!" *Plus, she made a great vroom-vroom noise.*

Singing Granny's praises failed to wipe the disapproval off Percy's face.

"We need a van," Ellis finally stated. "Park the van around the corner, throw the bike in the van, and profit."

"Profit how?"

"It's an expression."

Percy, to her great relief, went back to fidgeting. "Hm. A van *would* be handy. Unfortunately, we don't have one."

Ellis shrugged. "We'll steal one."

"Ellis—"

"We'll give it back!" she hastily replied. "It won't be grand theft auto, just…mediocre theft auto."

"Show me the line for *that* in the California criminal code."

"That won't come up because we won't get caught."

"Says the woman with the flawless bank heist plan," Percy grumbled.

Percy's genuine distress knocked Ellis out of the clouds. It was true. Her ultimately futile bank robbery had turned Percy into a wanted fugitive, effectively exiled to her apartment. Many of his animals lived here too, but occasionally, Ellis caught him staring at photos of himself beside an elephant or a lion at the zoo. She had decreased the size of his world.

"You can't become any *more* of a fugitive," Ellis pointed out, although she wasn't sure it would help.

His sigh ruffled the fur of a nearby long-haired cat. "I suppose you're right."

She grinned. "I'll shop for vans."

Two days later, she sat in a bright pink panel van emblazoned with the words TONYA'S MOBILE TAROT. The only thing new about the vehicle was the paint, and as the engine coughed to life, Ellis prayed to the Mother Beneath that it would last through the job.

"I don't like this." Percy climbed into the driver's seat wearing one of Ellis' black hoodies. He looked odd in that color. It was like seeing him out of uniform.

"I will admit the van is not inconspicuous," Ellis agreed.

"It's not that." Percy hesitated. "I just don't think we should rob a fortune-teller."

"Why not?"

"What if she called the police?"

"It's two-thirty in the morning. She won't know it's gone until tomorrow."

"What if she called the police *yesterday?*"

"I stole the van half an hour ago!"

"What if she *foretold* it?" Percy poked the velvet divider behind them. It featured hand-sewn pockets covered in arcane symbols in which nestled well-worn tarot decks.

"She's not a real psychic," Ellis argued. "If she were, she would have retired on her lottery winnings years ago."

"That's prejudiced," Percy retorted. "You didn't believe *I* was a real animal psychic, either."

"That's different!"

"How?"

"Animals have thoughts and feelings. They're not comprehensible to most humans, but they're real. The future doesn't exist!"

"It most certainly does, just as surely as the past. Covering your ears and saying 'Na na na na, I can't hear you' won't change that."

Pain spiked in Ellis' sinuses. Metaphysics was not her strong suit. It was time to leave before Percy made her headache worse. "It's too early in the morning to debate free will, Percy. However, it's the perfect time of day to rob the police. I'm *not* stealing another van."

Ellis thumbed open a glossy pamphlet she'd found on the dashboard. The cover showed a sharp-eyed redhead in a fringed blue hood whose eyes appeared to follow Ellis. "If 'Madame Midnight' had objections, she should have raised them yesterday."

Percy nodded as though that was wise instead of idiotic, and to Ellis' great relief, he started the engine.

The LAPD maintained several impound lots across Los Angeles, but finding out where Granny languished had been trivial. Their target was in a secluded area of Glendale, an ugly fenced rectangle between two strip malls that were as dark as death at this time of night. The orange sodium floodlights would normally have annoyed Ellis, but the upside to not having her shadow magic was that she didn't have to worry about it burning off.

They drove past the lot once to ensure it matched the satellite images, then looped back and parked beside one of the two strip malls. Percy retrieved his laptop and plugged it into a blocky, jerry-rigged device wedged between the front seats. Its battery weighed as much as Granny did.

"Mobile internet," Percy explained. "It steals bandwidth from every nearby source and combines it into a fast lane on the information superhighway."

Ellis smiled and nodded. Since she'd grown up in a cave, Percy's digital feats flew over her head at cruising altitude. "Impressive."

"It *is*," Percy grumbled. After several minutes of inputting incomprehensible on-screen code, six security camera feeds appeared in a grid.

Percy handed Ellis an earpiece. She slid it into her ear, and Percy leaned closer to a golf-ball-sized microphone clipped to the edge of the display. "Zookeeper to Black Cat. Come in, Black Cat."

The sound blasted Ellis' eardrum with the force of a typhoon, and she ripped the black plastic receiver out before it destroyed her sensitive hearing.

Percy winced. "That should have been the right setting."

"Not for me." He tilted his head in curiosity. *Let him wonder.*

After he turned down the volume, she slipped the earpiece back in. "Why am I 'Black Cat?'"

He ticked the reasons off on his fingers. "You're hard to see in the dark, you land on your feet, and you love to pretend you don't need other people."

"I *don't* need other people."

Percy smiled. "You remind me of my first cat. His name was Hex. He was a bastard."

That was obviously a glowing recommendation, so Ellis didn't argue. Instead, she opened the door. "I'll let you know when I'm in position."

"Copy that, BC." He hit three keys, and the camera feeds dissolved into static.

Ellis slipped through the shadows. Plastic sheeting covered the fence to shield the lot, but it was torn to shreds. Alas, she failed to pick Granny out of the rows of cars before the security gate came into view. She couldn't see the guard shack, and if she got any closer, they'd spot her, but she knew the small building and two officers were there.

"Percy, I'm here," she whispered.

"You're supposed to call me 'Zookeeper.'"

"Ugh. Fine. *Zookeeper,* I'm *here.*"

"Copy that, Black Cat. Launching Operation Old Lady."

"Rude!"

"I named it after the bike, silly."

Ellis' sensitive hearing picked up voices from the guard shack, and she shushed Percy. The camera feeds' failures had been noticed, and the cops were outside troubleshooting.

"It's not the power, or we would have lost the floodlights," one said.

"Shit. Let's do a circuit and check the wires."

"Should we call it in?"

"We're supposed to be off-duty in forty-five. If we call it in, we'll be here all fucking morning."

"Yeah, but—"

"But, nothing. Butt *out.*"

"Yes, sir."

Percy's whisper crackled into her earpiece. "Three, two, *one.*"

Ellis heard the explosion in her earpiece and ears

simultaneously. It was accompanied by brilliant white sparks that leaped into the sky like falling stars in reverse. Cheerful orange flames followed, and the acrid smell of burning rubber was close behind.

"What the fuck!" the guards shouted. They sprinted out a door beside the gate, service weapons drawn.

Ellis retreated deeper into the shadows and touched the bulletproof fabric of her long-sleeved black shirt. It wasn't as comforting as she'd hoped.

Percy had driven around for an hour before deciding which car was acceptable collateral damage. It was a junker, but the owner had excellent insurance, so when all was said and done, he would come out ahead.

Ellis was mildly alarmed that Percy had stored illegal fireworks in her apartment, but she wouldn't complain just now.

The chain link gate at the lot entrance clattered open with an electronic *whir* as the guards' footsteps receded in the direction of the burning car. Ellis sprinted through the gap and around the perimeter in a counter-clockwise direction. She passed trucks and sedans aplenty before spotting a plastic awning that blazed blue in the sodium lighting. Beneath was a fleet of motorcycles, some old, some new, some badly damaged.

Granny was in the middle.

The motorcycle's black paint gleamed, and comfort rushed through Ellis. Granny had been her lifeline for a long time.

Ellis had to fling aside two crotch rockets and one sadly out-of-place Vespa to free Granny. After the path was clear, she mounted the bike and popped the kickstand. She slammed the key into the ignition, tapped the gearshift to neutral, squeezed the clutch, and pressed the start button.

Nothing happened.

A light on the dashboard blinked, and Ellis cursed. She was out of gas. Granny's tank had been full when she'd abandoned her, so the police must have siphoned it off. *Shit.* She'd watched *The Great Escape* for nothing.

The exploding car would occupy the guards for a while longer. She still had time to run.

No. I won't leave you again, old girl. She stroked the gleaming black gas tank. Speedwalking out of an impound lot pushing a six hundred-pound bike didn't have the same flair, but it would have to do.

Ellis hissed into her earpiece. "Percy! I'm on my way, but the bike's out of gas. Pull up in front of the impound lot."

"That's risky."

"Our whole plan is risky!"

A long sigh. "Copy that, Black Cat. The sag wagon is en route."

Ellis dug her feet into the gravel and willed Granny to roll faster. Pink doors flashed by the gate as Madame Midnight's mobile tarot wagon rolled up, and while Ellis pushed the bike out of the lot, Percy opened the back doors.

An angry man shouted, "Hey!" and it was *not* directed at the abandoned burning car.

"We have to *move*," Ellis growled.

Percy unlatched the lightweight ramp, and it hit the asphalt. When Ellis rolled Granny onto it, it buckled and creaked.

"*Shit.*" Ellis tried to roll the bike faster, but the ramp cracked in half. Ellis caught the bike before it tilted and slammed into the pavement.

Percy made a noise under his breath that sounded like a squeak.

"What?" Even her sensitive ears couldn't hear everything.

"Sorry. Rat curse. Colorful vocabularies, rats."

Ellis had no time to think about it.

Granny wasn't the biggest bike Harley Davidson made, but all their bikes were large. Granny clocked in at around six hundred pounds.

Ellis could lift six hundred pounds if she had to. She hoped she could.

She leaned over and grabbed the chassis, and Percy's eyes widened. "You sure about that, girlie? First aid can't help a spine snapped in twain."

"I'll be fine." Ellis hoped she wasn't lying.

"Lift with your legs!" Percy uneasily advised.

Ellis wanted to shoot back a sarcastic "Thanks!" but she needed every wisp of breath. She drew three deep breaths, bent her knees, and lifted.

The worst part will be getting it off the ground. That thought replayed until the instant the tires left the ground, when it was replaced by "Uh-oh." Her quads burned and threatened to snap, and the tendons in her shoulders were white-hot with pain.

She pushed with her legs, and a *pop* made one knee wobble.

The bike inched into the air.

Percy grunted beside her. Even with him lightening the

load, they were at their limit. If her strength failed, Percy would be seriously hurt.

You won't fail. Come on, Ellis.

She hauled Granny up inch by inch until the front tire touched the floor of the van. The weight lessened significantly, and just when Ellis was sure she would black out, the bike rolled in. The floor swayed, but it held.

Sirens and shouting replaced the roaring of her pulse in her ears. Percy scrambled through the back of the van, over the bike, and into the driver's seat.

"*Get in!*" His voice, already high and thin, cracked with effort.

She hopped in and slammed the doors shut, and they barely latched before Percy stomped on the gas pedal. The acceleration flung her into the back window.

The van pulled a U-turn that made Ellis strain to keep Granny from falling over. She saw two figures sprinting toward them, backlit by the orange glow of the burning car. One leveled a gun at the van.

"*Drive!*" she screamed. A gunshot rang out, followed by a *ping* above her head. Then they were gaining distance, accelerating slowly under Granny's weight.

"Activate Plan Wily Diversion!" Percy shouted.

"I don't know what that is!"

"I'm talking to Flower! Also, don't most motorcycles have reserve tanks?"

A soft woof filtered through Ellis' earpiece as she spied the RES marking on her fuel valve. *Ellis, you're an idiot.*

She found out the next day.

A bland blonde with perfect mid-Atlantic intonation announced, "A crime spree at an LAPD vehicle impound lot led police on a wild goose chase, or should I say, a wild coyote chase?"

The newscast cut to police dashcam footage of a dozen coyotes blocking the road by milling back and forth across the asphalt.

A beaming Percy snapped a photo of the TV's screen with his phone. "I gotta tell Flower and the boys they made the news! They're gonna love this."

Ellis hoped she never ended up on Percy's bad side. She hadn't realized the extent to which humans shared the Earth with animals. "How do you know *so many* coyotes?"

"I make an effort," he primly replied.

"Well, thank you. For helping me commit crimes."

"Just do me a favor," he requested glumly. "Get that bike painted before they haul you in for riding stolen property."

Ellis assured him she'd handle it, then went back to staring at her door. Granny was covered by a drop cloth in the garage. Charlie would probably show up any minute to confront her.

Wouldn't he?

CHAPTER THREE

The straight-backed wooden chair was uncomfortable. A different spindle dug into Charlie's spine whenever he shifted. They'd receive complaints of "cruel and unusual punishment" about it if this was an interrogation room.

It could be worse. At least it's not contemporary art.

The captain's office had been transformed. The broad desk, antique hat rack, and certificates on the wall were gone, presumably retrieved by Jericho's surviving family, and an ergonomic stool had replaced the comfortable chair.

"Charlie Morrissey."

The man at the desk steepled his fingers. He was in no apparent hurry to talk.

A shiver ran up Morrissey's spine, but a jolt of pain from a spindle stopped it dead. Not talking was an interrogation technique. Meetings with Captain Jericho had felt like conversations rather than interrogations, but Jericho was dead. Morrissey would adjust.

"It's a pleasure to meet you, Captain." He crossed one

leg over the other, smiled, and waited. Two could play this game, and Morrissey was stubborn.

Captain Montgomery Irving's smile thinned. The man resembled a knife: thin and narrow-nosed, with steel-colored hair and sharp eyes. "I'd like to express my condolences."

Morrissey frowned. Had he missed something? "Sir?"

The smile disappeared. "I'd been led to believe that you and Captain Jericho were close."

Morrissey relaxed. Unfortunately, that put a different vertebra on a collision course with the evil chair. "Ah. Jericho was my mentor, yes. Thank you, sir."

Irving's suit didn't fit, and smudges marred his glasses. Did that indicate carelessness in his policing? It was too early to draw conclusions.

"I'm personally heading up the investigation into Jericho's death," Irving continued. "I want you to know that I will go to great lengths to bring his murderers to justice. Do you have any information to share about his death?"

Sure. I saw him shot point-blank by black ops agents prepared to deal with magical opponents. My vigilante friend threw gold bars at them.

"I'm sorry, sir. I don't."

Irving waited. Morrissey sensed he had formidable patience. The captain ought to buy a clock to *tick-tick-tick* the seconds off for his nervous suspects—if Morrissey *was* a suspect. The silence was maddening. *Well, let it madden* him.

Irving broke first. "Have you noticed anything unusual around the station?"

"Everyone's been on edge since Ron Jackson was fired."

That had the advantage of being true and boring *and* implicating Jackson. Morrissey wouldn't lose sleep if the dirty former cop went down for Jericho's death.

"That's understandable. Was Captain Jericho involved in Jackson's illegal operations?"

Unused to such blunt questions when it came to internal affairs, Morrissey jolted. The chair punished him with another jolt of pain. "From one cop to another, I understand why you're asking, but no. Jericho was a good cop. He held the center."

Irving's narrow face sliced the air in a curt nod. "I suspected as much. My next question? I don't know what you'll think of it, but I'll ask it anyway. Has anything supernatural happened recently, either here at the station or in Los Angeles at large?"

That was a hell of a surprise. Morrissey thought about Ellis and frowned. He and Ellis weren't on great terms anymore. What was Irving *really* asking? "Sir?"

The captain lifted a hand, palm-up. "I feel the same way about the question, but I've never refused to follow a lead, so I will ask you again. Were there any supernatural happenings around the station?"

Morrissey narrowed his eyes. "What kind of lead are we talking about?"

"I'm not at liberty to disclose my source." The captain smiled wryly. "Humor me."

What would throw Irving off Ellis' trail? *Not that she deserves a break.* "Ghosts," he eventually replied.

"Ghosts?"

"Yes. Jericho was worried about ghosts."

"Why?"

You see, sir, there's this raven-haired beauty... "I don't know, sir," Morrissey lied.

Irving's eyebrows almost touched during the following extended pause. Morrissey retracted his earlier idea about the clock. The silence was excruciating.

"Your name came up, you know," Irving commented.

"I assure you, sir, I am not a ghost."

The corner of Irving's mouth curled down in disapproval under his colorless eyes.

Tough room.

"Tell me about your pet vigilante."

"Ah."

What could he say about Ellis Burton? She had saved his life three times, she was cute when she blushed, and he hadn't talked to her since Jericho's murder.

Morrissey felt like he was standing at the end of a long line of dominoes, listening to tiles fall in the distance.

"I believed a vigilante was working in downtown Los Angeles, sir, retrieving snatched purses and so on," he replied. That much was true or had been a year ago.

"What are your thoughts about the downtown bank robbery?"

That worried Morrissey. Irving had barely been in his position for a week, and he was already drawing bright and *accurate* conclusions.

"I don't understand the security footage. It's weird."

That was half-true. Ellis was cute, but she was also strange. After he met her, Morrisey's life had strayed off the beaten path, without a doubt.

"I'm doubling the size of the team tracking Percy Rawlings," Irving informed him. "He was a lonely man without surviving family, so his disappearance isn't surprising. However, all his pets also disappeared, and according to his neighbors, he owned a dozen animals or more. I *don't* understand how a fugitive can haul a petting zoo around the country without being caught. He must feed them."

Morrissey hoped Irving would never have reason to examine his car, which was still full of loose hair and feathers. He *had* to get it detailed.

"What do you know about the impound burglary last night?" Irving asked.

Morrissey stalled. "What, the coyote debacle?"

"Yes. Also 'weird,' as you put it."

"No arguments there." The photos had creeped Morrissey out.

Irving rose. The man had so much capital-A Authority that Morrissey unconsciously rushed to stand.

Irving carried a glossy photograph to the wide, empty white wall that faced his desk and pinned it in the center.

It was Ellis. Irving didn't know that, but the blurred dark-haired shape in the printout from the security footage of the bank robbery was unmistakable.

Irving stepped back. The wall made a vast frame around the lonely photo. "This woman is my prime suspect in Captain Jericho's murder."

Morrissey demurred. "You think a woman did it? Jericho's death was violent."

"Women have an immense capacity for violence. They are only limited by opportunity."

Morrissey recalled several instances of Ellis fighting large men with more than pillows. "I'll keep that in mind."

Captain Irving nodded again, clearly in dismissal. "If

you think of anything else at any time, contact me. Here is my private cell." He handed Morrissey a plain white business card with a number printed in black ink.

That was unusual, but what worried Morrissey was the faint disapproval in his tone. Irving was suspicious. That could be his natural state. Morrissey didn't know.

As Charlie walked back to his office, he pulled out his phone, opened his contacts, and scrolled to Ellis' number. He should warn her about Irving's investigation.

Morrissey shook his head. Maybe it was time to disentangle himself and return to old-fashioned policing.

"Charlie!" His partner Liza Laponte came up behind him. She was cheerful. "What are you up to? Actually, never mind. Whatever it is, cancel it. I'm going for pho, and you're coming."

"Sorry, I can't."

"Don't be a buzzkill. Come eat a spring roll and gossip about the new boss."

Her gaze was wary above her bright smile. He could smell a hidden motive but had no idea what it was. Morrissey didn't think he could stand another interrogation today, even if it came with spring rolls.

"Rain check?"

The smile dimmed. "We've hardly had a chance to talk lately."

He winced. "I'm sorry, Liza, I have to...take Mr. Muffins to the vet."

Guilt dropped like an anchor in his gut as Liza's expression went from cajoling to worried. Mr. Muffins had let Liza pet his head *twice* before drawing blood. It was a world record, and it was among the reasons he trusted Liza.

Liza scratched the thin scar on her wrist. "Is he okay?"

"I dunno. I'll find out." The lie wrenched his small intestine, and he made a big show of looking at his phone. "Gotta go. I'm gonna miss my appointment."

"Yeah, of course. But, Charlie, we need to talk soon."

"We will. I promise."

Morrissey fled.

He picked a feather off the driver's seat and slid into his car. The exit presented him with a choice. Turning left would take him home. Turning right would take him to Ellis'. Neither promised a warm welcome.

The car behind Morrissey honked aggressively, startling him.

He turned left.

CHAPTER FOUR

Ellis pulled in between two cars, hopped off, and locked her bike. She was accustomed to concealing Granny with shadow magic, so having to find parking spots sucked big time. Surviving in LA without invisibility was horrendous. How did humans *do* it?

She retrieved a box from the hard case on the back of the bike, then ran a hand over Granny's new paint job.

Percy had suggested painting her neon pink. Ellis suspected he'd been planning coordinating outfits for when he rode pillion, but she had *gently* rejected the proposal on the grounds that neon pink was a touch conspicuous. The slate blue she had chosen shifted chameleon-like to match the sky. She liked it almost as much as the original black, and Granny didn't seem to mind.

Hector lived in a three-story apartment complex on the northern edge of Koreatown, complete with polished hardwood and Hollywood Regency lighting fixtures. There was one door on the top floor. *The penthouse? Nice.*

A bronze lion knocker roared from the red-painted door. Ellis knocked.

Hector opened the door and grinned. "Ellis! Come in!"

The penthouse had the same old-school charm as the rest of the building. Its windows looked out on the Hollywood sign, although it was barely legible from this distance.

Ellis removed a small plastic bag from her pocket and offered it to Hector. "I brought you a present. They're suncap mushrooms."

Hector's enthusiasm waned as he peered at the square white teabags in the clear plastic. "More mushrooms?"

"They're not hallucinogenic," she assured him. "They have a lot of vitamin D. If you're having lingering nightmares, making tea with them will help."

Ellis had struggled with nightmares until she'd forced herself to hang out on her balcony at noon. Not seeing spiders in every corner had been worth a sunburn.

Hector hesitated. "Thanks, but…"

"What?"

He looked away. "Never mind. You'll think it's weird."

If you only knew. "I won't, I promise."

"I *like* nightmares."

The declaration cast a new light on Hector's decor. The color palette included rich blacks and blood reds, and the furniture was all antique. The art on the walls…

Ellis approached a gilded frame that rose from floor to ceiling and enclosed a black-and-white woodcut of a sleeping woman. An indistinct shape loomed at the foot of the bed, so tall that its head bent sideways at the ceiling.

Ellis shivered.

Hector cleared his throat. "Yeah, uh, I had to move that one out of the bedroom. Too many dates complained."

Ellis' eyebrows shot up for several reasons, and she avoided looking at the blush on Hector's cheeks.

Nothing in his collection of brooding, frightening artwork was as unsettling as the woodcut, although a small glass figurine of a demon made her shiver again. She turned away from a glass cabinet of bat skeletons and ephemera, glanced through a doorway, and screamed.

A nude seven-foot-tall man was framed by the open door. His skin was taut over his overly defined tendons, and something was wrong with his face. She grabbed for the pools of darkness under Hector's curio cabinet but, as always, came away empty-handed.

Hector followed her line of sight and hurriedly assured her, "It's okay! It's a mannequin!"

Ellis' heart rate gradually decreased. The figure remained still, and when her brain agreed that he was telling the truth, she approached it.

Up close, the monster-man was rubbery, although unsettlingly lifelike. "Where did you buy this thing?"

"I didn't buy it. I made it."

He gazed at the monster as though it was a beloved child, and an alarmed *Why?* died on Ellis' lips. "Oh."

"I wanted to work in special effects when I moved to LA ten years ago. Building props and creepy monsters, you know. I took the job with Amelia to pay my bills while I worked my way up the ladder. She can be very persuasive, and not just because of the money."

That was true.

"Eventually, I squirreled enough away to go into effects

work full-time, but every time I tried to leave, Amelia gave me a raise. She found this place for me, too. I could never afford it as an artist."

"She has you in golden handcuffs."

"That makes it sound *fun.*"

Ellis made a show of inspecting a small oil painting of a demon and ignored her cheeks changing color to match the red velvet on the antique chaise beside it.

Hector's shoulder brushed hers. "The artist said he saw that in a well in Colorado."

Goosebumps marched across Ellis' skin in thin lines. "Then I'll stay away from Colorado."

"You don't seem like a girl who shies away from trouble."

"Trouble doesn't give me a choice."

Hector was standing too close. Ellis pushed past him to the doorway framing the monstrous mannequin and closed the door.

"It was creeping me out," she apologetically admitted.

"I consider that a high compliment."

Ellis flung herself on the chaise. "So, you *enjoyed* the hallucinations?"

Hector sank onto a black velvet club chair and put his feet up on the clawed ottoman. "'Enjoy' might not be the right word. I appreciate it in hindsight. Horror is a good way to encounter the full spectrum of the human condition without—"

"Being murdered by mole men?" Ellis had more in common with mole men than she'd like to admit.

"Exactly." Hector contemplated the demonic woodcut.

"What we experienced was terrifying, but it also made the world seem bigger. You probably think I'm nuts."

He crossed to a drafting table in the corner, pulled a sheet of paper off a pile, and handed it to Ellis. "When I came home after our adventure, I drew for the first time in years."

The highly skilled black ink drawing showed their mushroom grow-room crawling with dark figures. The spots on the rustcaps formed sneering faces.

"This is eerie," she told him. "It freaks me out."

That elicited a smile bright enough to cure nightmare node poisoning. "Thank you! Would you like to keep it?"

Not where I can see it when I sleep, she thought, but she unable to rebuff his obvious hope. "I'd love to."

Hector fairly bounced as he rolled up the drawing and slid it into a cardboard tube he retrieved from a desk drawer.

When he handed it to her, Ellis continued, "After the other night, I thought you might quit the mushroom project."

"Are you kidding me? You're the most interesting thing that's happened to me in years."

Those sparkling eyes were on her again. Ellis absent-mindedly stroked the red velvet and stuttered, "I-I'm glad you've taken an interest in mycology." *He didn't say he was interested in mushrooms, idiot. He said he was interested in* you. "I hope you don't make tripping on nightmare nodes a regular occurrence, that's all."

Hector shook his head, then blushed guiltily. "I did freeze-dry a few, but I don't plan on diving back in anytime soon."

"Good."

"In any case, if we don't fix the problem, Amelia will be furious. Even I can't get excited about that type of horror."

Ellis had glimpsed Amelia's temper. She had no desire to experience that shitstorm.

"Will we lose the whole crop? If so, we need to tell her sooner rather than later."

Ellis shook her head. "We can kill the nodes with high-intensity UV light. We'll lose some of the fruiting mushrooms, but we'll save most of the crop. Plus, now I have a taste-tester to ensure they're not still hallucinogenic."

Hector grinned. "At your service." He relaxed. It was telling that he was more afraid of Amelia than demons. "Speaking of hallucinogenic hellscapes, would you like to see a movie together?"

The corner of Ellis' mouth quirked up. "I'm not sure I would describe a date with you as a hallucinogenic hellscape."

"Oh, that's not, uh…"

While Hector stammered, Ellis wandered over to the drafting table. Any drawings of Amelia would contain clues about the Bromeliad's owner.

A mix of pencil sketches, ink drawings, and watercolor paintings sat in a messy stack on the table. The sketch on top showed a dark hallway with an elevator at the end. Its doors were cracked open a hair's breadth, but the viewer got the impression of something awful lurking behind.

"I'm not the hellscape. The movie is," Hector finally explained. "An experimental stop-motion horror animation is playing at the Vista next week. It's called *The Void of Arunak*."

Ellis flipped to the next drawing, which was a rendering of the LA skyline from the Bromeliad's roof. A horrific bird the size of an ostrich hunkered in one corner. One bulging eye burned into Ellis' soul. *Wormy!* Ellis wondered if the pigeon would be flattered or offended.

She tapped the paper. "Can I keep this one of the bird? I have a friend who'd love it."

"Agree to the movie, and it's yours," he flirtatiously replied, then sobered. "I'm teasing. I know you might have had enough horror for a while, but it's a rare thirty-five-millimeter screening, and I thought you might enjoy it."

Ellis slid aside the sketch of Wormy and froze. The next drawing showed Hector held aloft by a monster that was unmistakably Ellis.

She picked it up. The body of the Ellis-creature was distorted, and her raven's-wing hair formed a swirling void. Her blue eyes were milky, and a creepy smile twisted her face. She looked fundamentally evil.

Hector had seen her as a terrifying hallucination. He'd thought she was a monster, like the drow she'd grown up with.

More than you know, buddy. Tears stung her eyes. She blinked them away and abandoned the cardboard tube containing the mushroom drawing on Hector's desk beside the drawing of Wormy.

"I have to go."

Hector sensed the shift in atmosphere and came over to her. He spotted the terrifying drawing at the top of the pile. "Ellis…"

"I'm not a monster."

"I didn't say you were." Hector grabbed her arm as she

stormed past him, and she brushed him off with such force that he grunted in pain.

Ellis the beast strikes again.

"Wait, Ellis. It's just a drawing. I *like* monsters!"

There it was—his real opinion of her. He didn't like *her*; he just sensed what she was. His subconscious knew she wasn't fully human, and he was drawn to that. It wasn't a real rapport.

Ellis snatched the bag of suncap tea and slammed the door in his face.

She'd reached the stairs when she heard his voice through the door, thanks to her exceptional drow hearing. "Goddammit, Hector! You're such an idiot."

Ellis ignored Percy's concerned noises and stormed into her bedroom. A patient scratch at her door made her relent and allow Flower the pit bull entry, but she shut the door before Percy could horn in after her.

Ellis crawled into bed, pulled the linen-covered duvet up to her chin, and hunted for a movie on her laptop. Anything with a whiff of romance was rejected. Nothing appealed.

Ellis reluctantly typed in *The Void of Arunak*. It looked weird and unsettling.

Perfect for a freak like me. Ellis sighed, pushed Play, and curled into a ball.

A nose nudged Ellis' leg. Flower was looking at her with wide brown eyes.

"Ugh, fine." Ellis uncurled enough to admit the broad

gray head onto her lap, and Flower's tail wagged as she settled in.

Ellis turned out to be glad for the company. During a particularly alarming scene involving two children crossing a bridge over a snake pit, she stroked Flower's broad back. People often crossed the street to avoid the muscular dog when they were out walking. "People think you're a monster too, huh, girl?"

Flower woofed softly.

"I guess we're in good company."

It would have been stupid to get entangled with Hector anyway. He was deep in Amelia's inner circle, which meant he was, at best, a pawn. At worst, he was involved with the men who had killed Morrissey's boss.

When Ellis fell asleep with her head on Flower, her dreams were blessedly monster-free.

CHAPTER FIVE

The pounding of fists on wood broke through the velvety darkness.

Ellis shot upright, but Flower had only lifted one eyelid, so Ellis relaxed. If someone dangerous was at the door, her hackles would have risen.

The handle rattled. Then the strip of light under the door was swallowed by darkness. The door swung open, and her brother Landon waltzed in.

"Hey!" Ellis protested.

The golden talisman that made him look like a brown-haired human swung from his neck as he cheerfully waved. "You weren't answering. Needed to be sure you were okay."

"Don't pick my locks!"

Landon averted his gaze as he closed the door, then removed the talisman and deposited it on the bed. Purple spots appeared like freckles on his pale face, then spread until his skin was purple and his hair was silver.

"I, uh, didn't."

He stepped aside to reveal the quarter-sized hole through the knob.

"*Landon!*" Secretly, she was impressed. Landon's shadow magic was improving. Maybe he was finally relaxing enough to use his powers properly.

She sighed. "Did Percy let you in?"

"You wouldn't answer your door. He was afraid you were sick."

"I'm not." Ellis pulled the slate-gray duvet over her head, but Landon pulled it back off and banished the cave-like darkness.

"Knock it off, eggplant-face!"

"What?" Landon looked confused.

"I said, *knock it off.*"

"No. What did you call me?"

"Eggplant-face." It sounded stupid now.

Landon frowned. "What's an eggplant?"

Ellis glared. "An extremely ugly vegetable." *One of Percy's favorite foods.*

Landon was not bothered. "Oh, okay. You seem upset. What's wrong?"

She had no desire to confide her romantic hardships in her little brother. "Nightmare nodes."

Landon's gaze snapped to the door of her walk-in closet, which hid her personal grow room. He edged back.

"Not..." she stopped before she could finish with, "here." Landon didn't know about Hector and the Bromeliad. None of the dark elves knew she had brought their precious mushroom strains to the surface.

To be fair, Landon would likely consider it a petty crime and not have a problem with it, but if he told their

MARTHA CARR & MICHAEL ANDERLE

father? Connor would drag Ellis out of LA so fast he'd be a lavender blur.

"It's not a problem," she corrected. "I denatured and destroyed the infected mushrooms. It just made for a long week."

Fortunately, Landon wasn't keen to verify her claims. He threw himself down on the bed.

She pursed her lips. "What do you want?"

"Is that how you welcome your own flesh and blood? Who says I want something? Maybe I'm here to check on my little sister."

"I can take care of myself."

"Says the woman sulking in bed."

Ellis glared at him. Flower puffed up to her full height, ready to unceremoniously show the purple intruder the door on behalf of her pissed-off mistress. Ellis laid a hand on the dog's silver haunch, and Flower sat.

"I know that look," she told Landon. "You need something. Out with it."

Landon propped himself up on Ellis' brand-new pillows and got serious. "Errol's missing."

"Good riddance," Ellis retorted but softened when she registered her brother's dismay.

Errol had chosen to leave the drow homestead to live among humans. He'd claimed it was because the drow were too insular, but Ellis suspected he couldn't get along with anyone, dark elf *or* human.

Takes one to know one.

She pushed the uncomfortable thought away. It wasn't her fault she had skim-milk skin and round ears. Errol had mocked her aberrant features every time they'd met, which was usually when she was pulling Landon out of a mess Errol had created.

"He's my friend," Landon protested.

"Whatever trouble he's gotten into, he probably deserves it."

"I don't disagree with you, but I don't want him to die."

Stupid, loyal Landon. Even though they'd fought as kids, he'd been loyal to Ellis in his way. He never stopped teasing her, but if anyone tried to physically hurt her, he defended her in a heartbeat. He didn't understand that the teasing had been worse.

"When was the last time you saw him?" she asked.

"A month ago. He was living in the LA tunnels."

Why bother leaving the Swallow's Nest to go back underground? Ugh. Not her problem.

"We should start in the last place you saw him. I'll go down with you."

"He's not there anymore."

She frowned. "You said that was the last place you saw him."

Landon sighed and pulled something out of his gray silk pants.

"You have a *cell phone?*" Why was she shocked? It felt like Landon was usurping her connection to the human world—the connection she'd assumed was hers and hers alone.

Landon snatched it away before Ellis could grab it. He retrieved a cord from a different pocket and plugged it into the nearest outlet. "You have a phone. Why shouldn't I?"

"The homestead doesn't get service. Believe me, I tried."

"I don't use it at the homestead. Anyway, I haven't heard

from Errol in weeks. The last time we spoke, he was living…"

"What? Where?"

"You have to promise you won't tell Dad."

"I don't tell tales, Landon."

He believed that. Ellis kept her own counsel.

Landon rubbed his dark eyes with his palms several times and clutched his silver hair. "He's been living with some humans in Topanga Canyon."

Ellis frowned. "How does he recharge his medallion?"

Landon's reply was quiet. "He doesn't. He's living in the open, purple skin and all."

"*What?*"

Ellis could count the humans who knew about the existence of the drow on one hand. She was a staunch proponent for more integration with the human world, but Errol was *not* a stellar ambassador. *That idiot.* Even Landon wasn't stupid enough to reveal his true form to random humans. She was shocked that she hadn't heard about little purple men on the news.

"Is the homestead safe? Are the humans who know about the dark elves trustworthy?"

"They don't know he's a dark elf."

Ellis blinked. That statement bordered on incomprehensible. "Do they think he has a weird spray tan?"

"*No.* Mother Beneath!"

Landon unplugged his phone and poked it. Ellis recognized the slow and deliberate movements from her personal struggle with technology. After several *sotto voce* curses, he finally handed her the device.

"Whoa," she muttered.

The picture on the screen showed Errol with three of the most unusual people Ellis had ever seen. The man on the left caught her eye in particular. Tattoos of green scales covered every inch of his skin, and his eyebrows were lumpy hills. Implants, Ellis guessed.

"Who is that?"

"The Dragonman. They're all sideshow performers. They travel with circuses, attend art festivals, and busk in LA. Errol barely stands out."

"Huh."

Landon was right. Beside the Dragonman, Errol almost looked normal. On the drow's other side was a man covered in hoops, studs, and the occasional safety pin. Ellis hoped he didn't encounter many metal detectors.

The last person in the picture was a stunningly beautiful woman with extremely pale skin and white hair. Her eyes were pink. "She has albinism," Landon explained.

Ellis zoomed in to take a closer look at the heavy bracelets covering the woman's arms, but upon closer inspection, she realized they were coiled snakes. Ellis's gorge rose. She wasn't a big fan of reptiles.

"She's a snake charmer," Landon provided.

"She must get along great with Errol."

Landon leveled a disapproving look at her, and Ellis rolled her eyes.

She shifted her focus from the snake lady to Errol. Something was off about his appearance. It was hard to tell with his hair flopping around his face, but... "What happened to his ears?"

Landon looked disturbed and took the phone back.

"He had them rounded. His new crew knows a surgeon who doesn't ask questions."

Ellis' jaw dropped. She'd spent hours squishing her ears into points in the mirror at the homestead and imagining a life in which she looked "normal." Once upon a time, if the opportunity had presented itself, she would have signed up for that surgery in a heartbeat.

Now, the rounded ear below silver hair made her stomach turn. "Whatever Errol is up to, you should stay away," she told Landon.

"I was. Errol and I texted sometimes, but that was all." He hopped off the bed and crossed to the window, then stared out at the city Ellis had grown to know and love. "I'm surprised that you, of all people, would judge him for finding a place to fit in."

That arrow hit Ellis' sorest spot. She clenched her jaw. "Under other circumstances, I'd agree with you, but he almost got you killed more than once. Errol has stupendously bad judgment. You're much better off with him in your rearview mirror."

"My what?" Landon hadn't yet picked up critical car vocabulary.

Ellis groaned. "He belongs in your past. Look, Landon, we heard Nan Elandra's stories. Humans and dark elves *could* work together, but a petty criminal with sawed-off ears won't be the one to clear that cave-in."

Landon sat on the floor below the window and put his head in his hands. He looked so distraught that Flower padded over and licked his hand until he reluctantly scratched behind her ears.

"Please help me find him, Ellis. I can only do so much in

eight hours with the medallion, and you're better at shadow magic."

Ellis swallowed a bleak laugh. *Not anymore.*

"I want to know he's okay. That's all. If he hadn't helped me get here, I wouldn't be hanging out with you. I wouldn't understand you as well as I think I do."

Ellis couldn't shake the conviction that if she went after Errol, something terrible would happen. If it were only her life on the line, she'd risk it, but drow society was at stake. "No."

"I'd consider it a personal favor." Landon sounded like he was in pain.

"I'm *doing* you a favor," Ellis weakly protested.

Flower nuzzled Landon's downcast face.

"Traitor," Ellis muttered.

Landon's gaze shot up. "You're calling *me* a traitor? You're one to talk!"

"I was talking to the dog."

Her brother wilted again. "In that case, I need a favor."

"I already told you I'm not helping."

"A different favor. My medallion's out of juice. Can you walk me back to my bike in case I need to disappear?"

Admitting he needed help had to be driving him crazy.

She crossed her arms. "They're letting you drive a *motorcycle* in and out of the homestead? Things *have* changed since I left."

Landon chuckled wanly. "Not a motorcycle, a bicycle. And they're not *letting* me do anything. I hide the bike in the forest. I don't want to hear a whisper of objection unless you want to be the biggest hypocrite under the earth."

"Hmph."

He awkwardly got to his feet. "If you can disappear us that long, the medallion should last me the ride home."

Ellis' heart drained out through the soles of her feet. "Landon, I can't."

Hurt filled his face. "What's your problem? Do you think forcing me to use shadow magic in high-pressure situations will build character? Is this your idea of tough love?"

She groaned. "No. It isn't that I *won't* help you. It's that I *can't*. I'll explain, but you have to promise not to tell Dad."

He stopped glaring and sat again, then scratched Flower's ears. "I don't tell tales either," he stated quietly.

Ellis joined him by the wall. "Remember the men who tried to kidnap you with the lightsilk net?"

Landon shuddered and nodded.

"I ran into a group of them. I think it was them, anyway. I don't know for sure." She hoped it was. The idea of two groups equipped to fight drow was horrifying, although a single well-armed group fighting on multiple fronts wasn't much better.

Her photographic memory came in handy in situations like this. The events of Landon's kidnapping were as bright and fresh as a spring afternoon. The black Range Rover had been unmarked, and someone had removed its license plate. When Landon's legs disappeared as he fumbled with his shadow magic, three men had emerged from the black vehicle. Hoods shadowed their faces, and their clothes bore no distinguishing features. One pulled out a lightsilk net, and a familiar symbol glinted on a gold ring on his hand.

The half-moon with the two concentric circles.

Ellis gasped.

Landon nudged her arm. Her vision cleared to reveal his purple face lined with concern. "You had that faraway look."

"Something I remembered."

Landon was so worried he didn't roll his eyes in resentment about her perfect memory. "Something connected?"

"Yes. Now I *know* I ran into more men from the group who attacked you. They threw confetti at me."

Landon laughed, and Ellis' face burned. "It's not funny."

"I'm sorry, but...*confetti?* The invincible Ellis Burton, taken down by *confetti?*"

"It was lightsilk confetti."

Landon's laughter instantly died. "*What?*"

"It wasn't normal lightsilk, either. I haven't been able to use my shadow magic since."

"Lightsilk can last a few days."

"It's been a month."

Landon exhaled through his teeth. He hesitated, then put an arm around her. "I'm sorry, sis."

"No, *I'm* sorry. I'd help you if I could, but everything is much harder now."

"*That's* why you won't help with Errol."

Ellis paused. She wouldn't help Landon find Errol because his friend was an idiotic petty criminal who was bent on getting her brother killed, but if Landon thought she was licking her wounds, that suited her.

"I could help you," he told her.

Ellis cocked her head. "Don't tell me you've been spending time in the lab with Dad."

He made a face. "Mother, *no*. In the infirmary."

Ellis peered at Landon, looking for signs of illness. He *seemed* fine. "Looking for a cure for stupidity?" she teased. "Hope springs eternal!"

It was childish, and Landon ignored it, which made her feel worse.

"Do you remember the infirmarian who took care of me?"

Ah. Ellis elbowed him. "The gorgeous one?"

He blushed a darker purple. "Yeah. We've been spending a lot of time together. She knows almost everything about drow medicine, and what she doesn't know, she wants to." He finished by whispering, "She's better at mushroom compounding than Dad."

Ellis's eyebrows rose. Ellis believed Connor Burton was the only person who could help her, but he was the one person she could not tell. An equally skilled healer who was loyal to Landon was an interesting prospect.

"I won't tell her if you don't want me to," Landon offered.

Ellis pondered. "If you think she's trustworthy, you can tell her. I'm not making any headway by myself."

"I'll find out what I can."

"Thanks. I could drive you back to the homestead if you want," Ellis offered. "I gave Granny a new paint job."

"That's all right. I should fend for myself anyway."

Ellis sneaked his phone out of his hands.

"Hey! I need that!"

"You also need this." The phone wasn't locked. She tapped it.

Landon tried to see what she was doing. "What are you doing?"

"Adding my number." It was only half a lie. She *would* add her number—after she turned on location tracking. That way, if Landon went after Errol alone, she would know.

She pretended to struggle with the technology, then handed it back. "Call if you need anything. Buy a big battery block for it in case things get worse and I need your help."

Landon gratefully beamed at her, and Ellis struggled through a wave of guilt to return the smile.

CHAPTER SIX

Percy helped Ellis set her phone to alert her whenever Landon went into Los Angeles. It was a dirty trick, and she could feel the future fight in her bones. However, Landon had a prodigious talent for getting into trouble, and she knew the City of Angels better than he did.

She promised herself she wouldn't interfere unless he spent more than eight hours in the city. If the magic in his medallion ran low, she would check on him. Regardless, Ellis kept staring at the dot on the screen. She'd made it purple as a private joke.

He mostly stayed at the homestead.

Her phone beeped two days later, on Sunday afternoon. Without her magic, Ellis hadn't been patrolling much, so the alert was a welcome distraction. Ellis watched the purple dot appear at the edge of the Angeles National Forest, then continue moving at a speed that suggested Landon was on his bicycle.

Was he coming to visit her? He hadn't texted, but maybe... No, the purple dot went east, then north, past most of Los Angeles and into the San Fernando Valley. It wound up in the Malibu Hills.

Okay, Tour de France, where the heck are you going?

The answer was Topanga Canyon, which reminded Ellis of the picture of Errol and his new friends. Her brother *wasn't* keeping out of trouble, but if he stayed for two hours or less, he'd have time to make it home before his medallion died.

She put on F.W. Murnau's *Nosferatu.* When the titular character crept down the stairs, shadows bending behind him, Ellis wondered how much of human mythology the drow were responsible for. Had a drow inspired humans to invent vampires?

She snorted. Americans thought of elves as Gwyneth Paltrow types—willowy blondes surviving on air and sunlight. Dark elves were invariably portrayed as evil.

Ellis didn't *feel* evil.

You did rob a bank recently. Not a glowing contribution to the drow's optics.

Ellis grabbed her phone. What was Landon doing? It had been too long. More importantly, she was bored.

She stopped the movie and went to the garage.

Finding him was a good idea for multiple reasons. It was a beautiful afternoon. A cool breeze blew the haze off the hilltops and streamed Ellis' long black hair out behind her beneath her helmet as she rode north on the 101. She leaned into the corners in Topanga Canyon, driving as fast as she dared. This was why she refused to buy a car.

The purple dot was in an open field a quarter of a mile down the road from an overgrown turnout. Cars flattened every available inch of grass. Something was going on.

Ellis slowed her approach. Riding a motorcycle on gravel was perilous. When she was closer, a woman in a bright orange sweatshirt marked STAFF waved her down.

"Lot's full, but I'll let you park the bike if you promise not to block anyone in."

Ellis cheerfully nodded like she always did when she had no idea what was happening and crept into the field. The density of haphazardly parked vehicles increased, and keeping her promise to the woman at the entrance took a few minutes.

She finally found a spot to tuck Granny, and when the Harley's engine quieted, Ellis heard lively voices and music.

She followed the noise and discovered a large man in an even larger sweatshirt standing stock-still. On either side of him, rope wrapped around trees to create an informal corral, and beyond the partitioned space, a happy crowd gathered.

Long sideburns marched down the man's cheeks until they cascaded into tiny beards. A nametag identified him as "Maurice." He looked expectantly at Ellis' phone. "Ticket, please."

"Hey, Maurice. What's this about tickets?" Ellis ran her fingers through her helmet-dampened hair. A bright smile resolved many problems with men and rarely in their favor.

"You need a ticket. For the festival."

Ellis abruptly realized she was at a concert. "I don't have one."

Maurice crossed his arms. Ellis waited, but his only elaboration was a deepening frown.

She fished in her jacket for her wallet. "Could I buy a ticket?"

He snorted. "Sure. All you gotta do is build a time machine so you can go back to last December before the festival sold out."

Ellis groaned. "Come on, Maurice." She checked her pockets to see if she had anything to bribe him, but she suspected he wouldn't care about a vegan Korean takeout menu.

"Don't bother," Maurice told her. "I'm friends with the band and enemies with the fire marshal. You lose, lady."

She pointed to the crowd. "My brother's in there."

Maurice frowned. "How old is he?"

"Twenty-five."

Maurice snorted. "I think he'll be fine."

Ellis decided to take a truly *wild* swing. "How about I arm-wrestle you for it?"

Maurice was taken aback. Then, appraising her much shorter frame, he shook his head. "Nice try, but I won't be suckered into another personal injury lawsuit."

"What?"

"I know the score, sweetheart. We arm-wrestle, bones break, and lawyers get involved."

"If I break your arm, I promise not to tell any lawyers about it."

"Very funny."

"I'm stronger than I look."

An odd look grew in his eyes, the one Ellis often saw right before men stopped pulling their punches in a fight. Their survival instinct overrode their pride. Alongside it, however, doubt lingered.

Finally, he shot her a wicked, tobacco-yellowed smile and called over his shoulder, "Someone call Champ!"

Ellis raised an eyebrow, and Maurice chuckled. "I won't fight a lady, but Champ ain't got the same qualms."

Visions of an unscrupulous prizefighter flashed in Ellis' mind, someone with even more messed-up ears than her. The person who emerged from the crowd took Ellis by surprise.

Her initial guess hadn't been far off. Champ was six-two or six-three and built like a Mack truck…and Champ was a *woman*. Her high ponytail, which was secured with a black leather band covered in sharp spikes, increased her impressive stature.

Ellis gawked. She *really* wanted to ask Champ where she'd bought her scrunchy.

Maurice grinned. "If you beat Champ, I'll give you a VIP pass."

The imposing woman cracked knuckles covered in knotted, shining scars. "Oh, she's about to be a VIP, all right. A *victim in pain!*"

Champ sized Ellis up with a leisurely glance, then strolled away and pulled a keg off a nearby truck. She carefully placed it on Maurice's low table before banging her elbow down and leering at Ellis.

Ellis pushed the weightlifter's hand over the side of the keg so quickly that some of the onlookers missed it.

"What the fuck?" Champ stared at her hand in horrified indignation, then glared at Ellis and flexed her fingers.

Maurice's calculating expression changed to vindication. "Huh."

Ellis smiled. "You mentioned a VIP pass?"

He grunted, then told Champ to watch the gate and beckoned Ellis into the nearby security shack.

Soon afterward, Ellis triumphantly strode into the crowd, decked out in a free T-shirt, a free hat, and branded sunglasses. Over her shoulder, she carried a bag containing six Blue Thunder-flavored hard seltzers.

A brutal argument rang out behind her.

"You set me up!"

"Nuh-uh. If anything, she set us both up."

"Who is she?"

"A very important person...*ow!*"

"She must be juicing."

"You'd know better than me."

Ellis grinned as loud fiddle music drowned them out.

My first concert. She had nothing approaching a handle on human music. When someone asked her what she liked, which wasn't often, she had learned to name one band and stick to her guns.

According to Ellis' premium T-shirt, hat, and canvas tote, the band onstage today was the Aberdeen Connection. Ellis wasn't sure what they were connecting. Fiddles and beards?

Drow music was made for their acoustically perfect underground caverns and featured subdued melodies and stark arrangements. Lots of vocals, few instruments. Nothing about this band was subdued.

It included four fiddlers, two banjo players, two vocalists, a woman with a tambourine, and someone playing an instrument called a sackpipe. Or was it a bagflute? The contraption was prominently featured on her T-shirt.

The glassy-eyed crowd was packed into the corral as

tightly as the band was on the stage. Ellis felt claustropho-bic. Such a press should have been impossible under an open sky, yet Ellis' breath sped up.

Calm down. You can always punch your way out. She was strongly considering doing so when someone grabbed her shoulder and made her drop her swag bag. A glint of gold stopped her fist in mid-air.

A round medallion the size of a coffee cup with curling whorls that mimicked the underside of a mushroom hung beneath an olive-skinned face that shrank back from her fist. The woman to whom it belonged had long, straight hair and honey-colored eyes.

"What are you doing here?" The woman sounded weirdly familiar. "Have you been following me?"

Ellis recognized the aggravated tone from a hundred arguments. "*Landon?*"

Someone echoed her shout. "Landon?" This voice was deep, but Ellis recognized the drow lilt, as well as the pale face and floppy brown hair. An identical medallion hung around the man's neck.

"*Lanny!*" The man glared at the olive-skinned woman.

The woman hushed them both sharply. "I'm trying to lay low!"

"I've seen birds lay lower," Ellis muttered accusingly. Then, she poked the talisman around the newcomer's neck. "Who are you? Errol?"

"Errol? Lanny, why would she think I'm *Errol?* Mush-rooms wouldn't grow on that boy's dead body." The voice, though still deep, was painfully and possessively feminine. The contrast hurt Ellis' brain.

Landon winced as Ellis turned a searing glare on him. "Who's this, *Lanny?*"

The brown-haired man stuck out a hand. "We've met, actually. I'm Trissa."

Ellis' face broke into a gleeful grin as she shook. "You're the new *girlfriend.*"

Trissa's answering grin stretched her five o'clock shadow, and she leaned in conspiratorially. "Did he really call me his girlfriend? Did he use that *exact word?*"

Landon attempted to shrink into the crowd, but Ellis grabbed him by the collar. "Oh, no, you don't."

"Catfight!" a man jeered behind her.

"Somebody find some mud!" This came from a scrawny, shifty-eyed man who ran a wet tongue across chapped lips.

Revolted, Ellis released her brother's collar.

Landon looked mystified, then stepped close to Trissa and whined, "Can we please switch back?"

Trissa poked him in the chest. "No! You agreed."

Ellis narrowed her eyes. "Is this a sex thing?"

"No!" Landon blurted. Trissa scratched her chin thoughtfully. "*Triss!*"

"What? I'm giving the question fair consideration!"

Human Landon was capable of blushing, and he was doing his best impression of a tomato. Ellis couldn't keep the grin off her face. *Well, well, well, little brother. How the tables have turned.*

"We were wearing the medallions normally," Landon explained, "but Trissa insisted that people were treating her weird, so I told her I would switch." His stance was too wide and his movements too clunky for the feminine frame.

Meanwhile, Trissa was admiring her left bicep. "You didn't say you would switch. You said you would prove me wrong."

A man pushing toward the stage elbowed Landon aside and grazed Trissa's shoulder. "Oh, sorry, man." Then he disappeared into the throng.

Landon's jaw dropped. "He practically pushed me over! Why did he apologize to *you?*"

Trissa flexed again. "I bet Ellis understands!"

Unfortunately, Trissa was right. It had been among her first lessons.

As a rule, drow men did not harass drow women if they ever wanted to see one again, and you didn't touch a shadow mage without enthusiastic consent if you enjoyed having hands. Similar to humans, drow men tended to be physically stronger, but unlike humans, drow women frequently had stronger shadow magic.

Fortunately, that had resulted in peace rather than mutually assured destruction.

Human society was different, and for the most part, Ellis had become accustomed to it. No one harassed her twice, in any case.

Ellis beamed at her brother. "Put on your big girl panties, Landon. You'll survive. If you manage to leave in time, that is." She glanced at the timer on her phone. "You don't have much time left on your medallions."

Landon narrowed his eyes. "How would *you* know?"

Damn it. She'd distracted him, but she couldn't hold off the hard questions forever.

The music wheezed to a halt, and a woman with red pigtails stood on tiptoe to speak into the mic while the band members slumped and wiped their faces with tartan handkerchiefs. "Ladies and gentlemen, that was *Grass in the Wind*. We'll take a five-minute break and be right back with more."

Landon wasn't deterred. He crossed his arms. "Why are you here, anyway? *Have* you been following me?"

"No!" Ellis protested. She was *tracking* him. It was totally different.

She scrambled for an explanation. What had possessed her to barge in the front entrance? There had to have been an easier way to keep an eye on her brother.

"Am I not allowed to enjoy the...the..." she glanced at her chest, "the Aberdeen Connection?"

"Big fan, huh? Name a song."

"*Dust in the Wind*," she said primly.

"It's *Grass in the Wind*."

"That one, too."

Landon opened his mouth to launch into another tirade, but Trissa interrupted by tugging on Ellis' sleeve. "You have an *admirer*?"

Ellis followed Trissa's gaze. The high ponytail with the spikes was moving toward them like a shark fin slicing through the water. "That's Champ! She got me my VIP pass."

Champ pushed two young women aside as she barreled toward the trio. They looked like they considered protesting, then got an eyeful of Champ's biceps and scattered. "Champ giveth, and Champ taketh away," the woman intoned.

"Hello, Champ," Ellis said.

"Only my friends call me Champ." She rubbed her right hand, which was still red where Ellis had gripped it.

"Oh, pardon me. Hello, Champion…ess?"

Landon snorted. Triss scoffed in disapproval. Champ was silent.

Then, she sucker-punched Ellis in the stomach.

"Catfight!" the man from before called, but the cheer died in his throat when Champ snarled at him. This time, no one called for mud.

Ellis' lips formed several words: "Ow," "Stop," and "Good one," but no sound came out of her mouth. Her diaphragm had been knocked out of commission, and like the crowd, she was struck dumb.

Trissa stepped in with her fists raised. "Hey! Stop that!"

The crowd saw a man coming at a woman with his fists up. Ellis knew it wouldn't matter that the woman in question was capable of defending herself, nor that the man in question was actually a woman.

Ellis reached for her brother's girlfriend, but it was too late. The disguised drow woman delivered a forceful punch to Champ's jaw.

The man who had advocated for girl-on-girl mud wrestling moments earlier dug some outrage out of his depleted conscience. "He just hit a woman!"

The silence shattered into an uproar as eight men spun on Trissa.

Look! Chivalry!

Ellis loved chivalry. Men were surprised when she hit them.

Trissa realized her mistake and muttered, "Oh, shit."

She reached for the shadows below the crowd's feet, and three wisps of magic floated toward her fingers, but they dissolved in a useless puff when she lifted her hands to guard her face.

Ellis grabbed a short, beefy man barreling toward her and threw him at another attacker about to strike. The two men tumbled to the ground and brought a third brawler down with them. The three bodies formed an effective barrier on Trissa's right.

Their left flank was still open, and three more men pressed in. Landon grabbed the ankles of a man in a yellow beanie and flung him into the crowd. The concertgoers caught the human projectile, and the man's alarm turned to confused protest as he was crowd-surfed away.

Ellis was sizing up a tall man in a Rams jersey when the cacophony surrounding the fight died. Her opponent looked over her shoulder in confusion and fear, then joined the people clearing a wide circle in the pit.

In its center lay Trissa, as purple as a lilac in bloom, and beside her stood a short, bulky man in a Dodgers cap. Trissa's golden talisman dangled from his right hand, and the frayed ends of the snapped leather cord swayed in the late afternoon breeze. The man choked and dropped the talisman on the grass.

Trissa's electric blue eyes wildly rolled from side to side as she assessed the level of danger.

"It's a lady!" someone shouted.

Champ advanced through the crowd by sheer force of will. "No. It's a monster."

Metal gleamed as she slid a set of brass knuckles onto

her hand. Trissa reached for the shadows, and Champ dove.

Landon tackled her before her fist could connect with Trissa's face, and Ellis leaped forward and kicked the Amazonian woman in the gut. Champ's breath exploded in a satisfying hiss as she crashed to the ground.

Trissa and Landon stood back-to-back, and Ellis joined them, swinging her bag of seltzers at anyone who stepped toward them. The frightened shouts and snaps of camera shutters were increasing in both volume and frequency. The balance between fight and flight would tip soon, but either outcome would be dangerous.

A fleeing crowd can kill you as easily as assailants.

A sullen face with sunken gray eyes and yellow teeth sneered. The man held a glass beer bottle aloft as he considered Ellis, Landon, and Trissa. Ellis suspected he was deciding whether to uphold his earlier injunction against hitting women.

He licked his lips and broke his bottle on a trash can.

Oh, shit.

A shout cut through the din.

"LAPD! Freeze!"

The order parted the crowd enough to allow a plain-clothes officer through.

Ellis froze for two reasons. One, the man had a gun. Two, it was Charlie Morrissey.

When Charlie saw Trissa, he inhaled loudly in the sudden hush. He didn't look angry or shocked but exhausted like a camel being loaded with more straws.

"Take the mask off!" he shouted at Trissa. Then, his gaze met Ellis'.

Cold fear crept up her limbs. "It's not a mask," Ellis whispered.

Charlie looked closely at Trissa, and Ellis thought the dark circles under his eyes deepened a shade. He knew it wasn't a mask, and that terrified him.

"It's...face paint," Ellis offered. Charlie wouldn't believe it, but the crowd might.

One woman loudly proclaimed, "It's a marketing stunt!" and murmurs of agreement and disagreement fluttered through the mob.

Mercifully, Charlie rolled with it. "Okay, Miss Cosplay, up you get." He hauled Trissa to her feet and reached for his handcuffs.

Trissa tensed when she saw the gleaming silver, but Ellis frantically shook her head, and fortunately, Trissa noticed. She raised an eyebrow, and Ellis nodded toward the exit.

Trissa allowed Charlie to cuff her and lead her away.

Landon leaned into Ellis and murmured, "Who is that?"

"A friend," Ellis whispered back.

"Friends don't arrest friends," Landon hissed.

They do if we want to get out of here. "You don't know Charlie Morrissey. Come on." Ellis threaded after their retreating shapes.

She didn't understand why she was standing up for the policeman. Why was Morrissey here? He had no right to follow her.

Said the pot to the kettle.

Charlie's body language was scrupulously relaxed as he pushed the lilac-tinted woman out of the concert area. When he thought no one was looking, Ellis saw him sniff his water bottle, no doubt wondering if someone had spiked it.

Charlie brought Trissa to an unmarked police car in the labyrinth of parked vehicles. Ellis and Landon caught up as Charlie swung the back door open and practically shoved Trissa in.

"Where's your partner?" Ellis demanded.

Charlie pressed his lips into a thin line and said nothing.

Ellis sighed. "Come on, Charlie. You can let Trissa go."

"Oh, *can* I? Is that your recommendation, based on your many years of experience as an officer of the law?" His fist had white knuckles, and Ellis had to step back from his sprayed spittle.

"Mother Beneath, don't be an ass," she muttered.

"Mother *what*?"

Ellis reached for the handle of the car door. "Charlie. Seriously. She's my friend."

He pushed her hand away. "All *that* tells me is that she consorts with known criminals."

"What? Known to who?"

"To me!"

"I'm not a criminal."

"Did they pass a law making it legal to rob banks when I wasn't looking?"

Ellis glared. Yes, she'd robbed a bank, but she'd done so to save them from Ron Jackson's blackmail. "I did that to protect you."

"You did it to protect yourself."

"If all I wanted was to protect myself, I would have just disappeared."

Out of the corner of her eye, Ellis saw Landon and Trissa exchange looks through the window of the patrol car. Trissa angled away from Charlie and Ellis and stretched her cuffed hands toward the darkness under the front passenger seat. Shadow magic looped around her slender fingers.

Ellis smirked. She had no intention of intervening in whatever Trissa was planning. Charlie was being a grade-A jerk.

Charlie pointed at Landon. "You're under arrest too, missy."

"Charlie—" Ellis began.

Charlie cut her off with a glare. "That's 'Detective Morrissey' to you."

He opened the car door again and shifted his weight onto his toes as though he was anticipating a struggle. Landon shrugged and clambered into the patrol car.

When Morrissey slammed the door behind him, Landon tried the handle, but it wouldn't open from the inside. Trissa yanked his arm away. She'd already freed her hands.

Time for a distraction. "What are you doing here?" Ellis asked.

"Protecting the public peace, apparently," Charlie replied dryly. He added, "Ellis, who is that? Why is she purple?" His tone shifted from demanding to plaintive. Ellis realized he was frightened.

Ellis, fully aware that it was hopeless, tried to reassure him. "Don't...don't worry about it."

His glare was so withering that Ellis' throat went dry.

She retrieved a hard seltzer from her bag and popped it

open. Ginger ale and vodka sprayed her, and she sputtered. "What the *hell!* Is it *supposed* to do that?"

"That's what happens when you beat on someone with a bag of carbonated beverages." Morrissey's tone implied that she had missed a critical point in the human experience.

Ellis dropped the overflowing can, and Morrissey raised an eyebrow. "Adding littering to your long list of crimes, I see."

"We both know you won't arrest me. Let my friends go, and I'll tell you what I can."

Morrissey snorted. "Not until you give me some names. Start with the girls in the car."

He tapped a nail on the back window once, then again.

After the third tap, screws groaned, the glass darkened, and the car's roof exploded. A thick disc of shadow pushed through the roof and dissolved into the twilight, and metal splinters rained.

To his credit, the shards had not settled before Charlie flung the door open to check on Landon and Trissa. "Are you al—"

They were gone.

Charlie made a strangled noise, certain they'd been blown up, but the back of the car was pristine apart from the metal and glass carnage.

Ellis saw the blades of grass in the next field bend under two pairs of feet.

She yanked Charlie back before he cut himself. "Charlie! It's okay. They're fine."

"But, the explosion!" He threw open the front door and

grabbed his radio, only to swear when it came off in a mess of severed and melted wires.

Ellis put her mouth beside his ear and murmured, "You know how I can dissolve metal?"

He stilled. "You did this?"

"No. What I'm saying is that I'm not the only one who can."

Fear filled his eyes.

Yeah, fair. I'm the boogeyman.

She had wounded Charlie's pride when she hadn't wanted him to know what she was. He had resented that she'd kept him at a distance, but now that he had seen a full drow in person, Ellis felt vindicated. His horror at Trissa's lilac skin was burned into her memory.

"I need an explanation before I call for backup."

"Sucks to have unmet needs."

His hand clenched on the jagged edge of his patrol car, and a sliver of metal dug into his finger and drew blood. There was a hint of a curse in his grunt. Then, he pushed off the car. "That's how you want to do this? Fine. Ellis Burton, you're under arrest."

She was so shocked that she didn't respond to the cold steel locking around her wrists. "What are you doing?"

"For once? My job."

"You think these cuffs can hold me?" She let her gaze drift toward the roof of the car. He didn't need to know it was a bluff. As far as Morrissey was concerned, she could disappear whenever she wanted to.

"You do what you have to do. I'm doing what I have to do."

The metal dug into her wrists. "Ow," she muttered. Charlie's gaze softened.

A bird chirped nearby. Ellis kicked herself. She should have clapped her hands above her head before Charlie cuffed her.

"What now?" she asked.

"I wait like a chump until you disappear. Tough work, but I'm an old hand."

Ellis sighed. "You'll wait a long time. I can't disappear."

He twitched in surprise. She shifted her wrists.

After a couple of minutes, he said, "You're telling the truth." He'd evidently been banking on her escaping. Now he was the dog who'd caught the car and didn't know what to do with it.

"That stuff I got shot with at your boss's house? It never wore off."

"Are you okay?" His concern felt like too little, too late.

"How would you feel if you lost your hearing or your sense of taste?"

"Not great."

"Ditto."

Morrissey scrubbed a hand over his face. "Ellis, please. Who was that purple woman? Give me a name, and I'll let you go. Just a name. I don't even need an explanation."

She glared at him. "You asshole. I told you what was happening so you could help me, not so you could black-mail me."

"A *name*, Ellis."

"No!"

"Fine. Then enjoy jail." He rifled through the glove

compartment for a backup radio, but he didn't look thrilled at the prospect.

"You're way too trusting, you know."

Morrissey raised an eyebrow.

"You're assuming I won't rat you out for all our meetings the second the cell door clanks shut."

"Are you threatening me?"

"No. I just want you to understand why I have to do *this*."

She spun and kneed him in the guts. Morrissey deflated, half from the blow and half from surprise. She leaned on the patrol car to keep her balance, then kicked his legs out.

"I said I didn't have powers," she shouted back as she raced for the trampled spot in the grass and prayed that Trissa hadn't dragged Landon halfway back to the drow homestead by now. When the air cooled, she knew she hadn't. "I never said I didn't have friends!"

She stepped into Trissa's envelope of shadow magic and disappeared.

Morrissey stared after her. His disconsolate expression was depressingly familiar, but the pain on his face was mingled with disgust.

Ellis felt sorry for him, but she could deal with that later.

She turned to Landon and Trissa. Landon had taken his talisman off, and they were holding hands—the perfect drow couple. She resisted the urge to gag.

Ellis awkwardly retrieved Trissa's gold medallion from her pocket and tied the snapped cord in a hasty knot. "Here."

The talisman disappeared into Trissa's pocket. "I appreciate your help. We would have been in a *lot* of trouble."

"You're not out of the woods yet." Ellis looked out of the envelope of shadow magic toward the parking lot. Morrissey was facing the highway and heard distant sirens wailing.

Ellis lifted her wrists. "Can you help me with these?"

The link between the cuffs dissolved at a touch of the drow woman's finger, and Ellis sighed. "Thanks. You know, you didn't have to wreck Charlie's car. I don't know how he'll explain that."

"Charlie? You *know* that human? I thought he might harm us."

Ellis shook her head. "Not if he could help it. We should go."

Ellis retrieved Granny with Trissa's help. The big Harley joined them in the tent of shadow magic.

"I can't fit two of you on the bike," Ellis said apologetically.

"That's fine. By the time our medallions wear off, it'll be past dark," Landon replied.

They had stashed their bicycles under an oak tree. While Trissa checked them, Ellis turned to her brother. Her adrenaline was wearing off, and she was tired. "Why were you even here today? What were you doing?"

Landon shrugged. "I like the Aberdeen Connection. Errol and I used to listen to them. We snuck into a few concerts. Some of Errol's new sideshow friends were here, and I was planning to ask about him. Start tracking him."

Trissa smacked him on the shoulder. "You said you wanted to introduce me to your favorite band!"

Landon held up his hands. "I did! I was multitasking. They don't have bluegrass at the homestead."

Ellis snickered. "They'd have to call it 'purplegrass.'"

Neither Landon nor Trissa laughed. Ellis shrugged and threw a leg over Granny's black leather seat. "Get home safe," she told them, then revved the engine.

Trissa and Landon slipped their medallions back over their necks and appeared to be human.

"Thanks." Landon pushed off and pedaled away. "And stop following me!"

CHAPTER SEVEN

Charlie wearily rubbed his eyes and read the same line on the claim form for the seventh time. The memory of Ellis' face as she'd popped out of existence was playing on repeat in his head. She'd looked smug rather than remorseful, but she wasn't a sadist. She'd probably feel sorry for him if only for the sheer amount of paperwork he had to do.

He gave up on the form and went back outside. The insurance adjuster was examining the umbrella-sized hole in the roof with a magnifying glass.

"You described this as a 'malfunction,' Detective?" The adjuster's tone made it clear that he didn't believe a word of Charlie's story.

"The function of a car's roof is to protect passengers from the elements. Mine doesn't. Seems like a malfunction to me."

"It looks more like you got hit by a…" His voice trailed off. When he couldn't come up with a better explanation, The adjuster sighed. "Repairing it would be pointless." He promised to follow up in a few days, and Charlie went back inside.

Mr. Muffins had commandeered his desk chair, which Charlie happily accepted as an excuse not to continue fighting with the insurance claim. When someone knocked on the door a minute later, Charlie assumed the insurance adjuster had forgotten something.

He had not. Liza Laponte stood on his front porch with her arms crossed.

Charlie awkwardly glanced at the wrecked car parked on the street. "Liza. Hey."

She pushed past him without waiting for an invitation, which annoyed Charlie, although they'd never stood on ceremony before. "Do you have coffee?"

He'd emptied the coffee pot an hour ago, but he made a new pot while Liza followed him around the kitchen and agitatedly threw open cupboards and fiddled with mugs. When he finally handed her the pot and ushered her into a chair at the kitchen table, her foot tapped the floor.

Mr. Muffins paused in the open doorway, his prey instincts having been engaged by the movement. Morrissey glared until the orange cat padded away. Today was not the day for bloodshed.

"What happened to your car?"

"Every man has a midlife crisis and buys a convertible. I can already feel the wind in my graying hair…"

That further soured Liza's bad mood. She pulled a slim laptop out of her crossbody bag and set it on the table with a threatening *thump*.

"We've been partners for five years, and until a few months ago, I trusted you." In one sentence, Liza blazed past the chitchat with which Morrissey was hoping to redeem himself.

She levered the laptop open and pivoted the screen toward him. Green text covered the screen in a throwback to the earliest era of message boards. The URL read **thetruthfairy.com**.

"The *truth fairy?*"

"The web crimes division monitors this site. It's ninety-nine percent loony, but sometimes they find a diamond in the rough." She scrolled down, then pointed at a post.

"Evil scientists control the government?" The post insisted a secret society was controlling the USA via underground experiments.

"Not that one. The one below it."

"Little blue men?"

"Little *indigo* men. Aliens at a bluegrass concert."

Shit. Liza had found something legitimate. He shifted in his chair, uncomfortable with the conversation's direction, and tried to deflect. "*Aliens* are your diamond in the rough?"

"The post is garbage. I'm interested in *this*." Liza zoomed in on a small image, then watched Charlie closely.

It was a photograph of him. Rather, it was a photograph of him marching a woman with purple skin, ash-gray hair, and pointed ears through a crowd.

"What the fuck is happening, Charlie?"

If she only knew how frequently Morrissey asked himself the same question.

"It's probably photoshopped," he weakly suggested.

"It's not," Liza bluntly refuted. "The geek squad flagged it *because* there's no evidence of digital alteration. Then they ran a background check on the camera's owner. He's a sixty-five-year-old woodworker from Topanga Canyon who got a smartphone to look at photos of his grandkids, not a tech guru with access to fancy apps."

"Then it's a hoax."

"I would have believed that until *real* recently, but you've been keeping secrets from me. I still don't know why you're staking out that downtown apartment complex, but if it was legitimate, you would have asked me for help." She sounded more sad than angry.

That was Ellis' apartment. Liza had been following him.

"A lot is happening," he tried.

"Tell me."

"Liza, I can't. It's dangerous, and you wouldn't believe me anyway."

"*Please* don't tell me you believe in aliens."

He was about to say, "No, of course not," but the words died on his lips. *Could* the purple-skinned woman at the Aberdeen Connection show have been an alien? Was *Ellis* an alien? It was a crazy thought, but her powers of invisibility and hand-slicing were crazy too.

"I... No. I'm not a UFO chaser."

He could tell Liza didn't believe him. That was fair. Charlie barely believed himself.

She crossed her arms. "Tell me what you've been up to, or I'll go to the captain."

"Jericho's *dead*," Charlie stammered.

Liza stared at him. "Not him. The new one. Irving."

"Oh. Right."

It was hard for Charlie to think of anyone else as "the captain." The change hadn't sunk in. If Irving was into

MARTHA CARR & MICHAEL ANDERLE

ghosts, he'd love hearing about aliens. He might be receptive to a conversation about little blue men...or big purple women.

Morrissey couldn't let that happen.

He raised an eyebrow. "What will you tell him, that someone's playing a weird joke on the LAPD? Who cares?"

"I'll tell him you're involved in something." Liza's posture betrayed her growing anxiety. She was losing confidence.

Guilt prodded Morrissey, but he pushed on. "'Involved in something?' If you go to a veteran with that, he'll have questions. *Detailed* questions."

"I'll tell him the truth."

"What truth?"

"The only one I have."

"I've already met one-on-one with the captain," Morrissey told her. Liza's mouth twitched, which told him she hadn't.

Morrissey's gut churned as he decided how dirty to play this. He hadn't gotten the sense that Irving was the kind of old-school cop who hated having women on the force, but Liza didn't know that.

"You can't tell a man cut from good ol' boy cloth about *aliens.* If he doesn't put you on psych leave, he'll laugh you out of the building. He'll be joking about the hysterical lady detective with his golf buddies in no time."

Feeling even guiltier, he twisted the knife. "Why do you think he only asked for a one-on-one with *me?*"

Liza's face stilled. "I've proven myself to a thousand assholes. I can prove myself to one more. And don't talk to me about golf. I have a better handicap than half the department."

"He would have to invite you to find out."

Just before her gaze calcified into the flinty, unreadable stare she used on suspects, he saw a flash of pain. He'd hurt her feelings with that potshot, and relationships didn't always recover from those. Worse, it hadn't been true.

She ignored him, finished her coffee, and stood. Morrissey moved to follow, but she shook her head. "I can find my own way out of this shithole."

It was a fair summary of her attitude as a detective.

"I'm watching you, Charlie. You'll slip up eventually. I won't let you become the next Ron Jackson without a fight."

Charlie deserved that, but it hurt.

His partner and erstwhile friend walked out the door without another glance. Mr. Muffins padded after her, then paused and glanced at Morrissey.

"Leave her alone."

Mr. Muffins meowed and hopped up on the table in an elegant motion. He sat at the opposite end and licked his paw approvingly.

"If *you're* on board, I *am* an asshole."

Morrissey sighed, then reached across the table to pet the cat. His bright orange paw flashed out and he yowled, and Morrissey pulled his hand back with a yelp.

He cradled it and examined the blood welling in the scratches. "I deserved that."

Mr. Muffins meowed.

CHAPTER EIGHT

Ellis woke from her favorite new recurring dream where she sat inside an impossibly bright prison cell while Charlie Morrissey walked away. She *thought* it was him, anyway. She couldn't see his face, only his silhouette through the bars as he retreated down the empty white hallway.

She was angry. Angry about Landon's carelessness, Charlie's callousness, and Trissa's effortless use of shadow magic.

Her anger prickled under her skin as she spritzed the mushrooms in her shoe closet. Eating a nightmare node would be better than feeling claustrophobic in her own skin.

At three in the morning, after abandoning an attempt to clean her apartment floors—a Herculean task thanks to the animals in residence—Ellis donned black jeans and a black turtleneck, stashed her utility belt in a deceptively large bag, and rode Granny to the Bromeliad.

In the elevator, she hit the button for the first floor, then the penthouse. She disembarked on the first floor and took the stairs down to sub-basement two. Unless she was unlucky, the elevator would stay on the penthouse level while she worked.

The stairs didn't go to sub-basement three. That was odd and probably a fire hazard, but it was also enticing.

Ellis retrieved a moonsteel bar with a tapered end from her bag, wiggled it between the elevator doors, and pushed. The door mechanism was strong, but she and the moonsteel were stronger, and the doors popped open.

Ellis glanced up the dark shaft. If the elevator came down, she'd be paste, but she doubted anyone would use it at four in the morning. If they did, it was unlikely they'd go to sub-basement three.

She swapped the moonsteel jimmy for her new grapnel and hefted it. It was lighter than her old one and untested. *Only one way to find out if it works.*

She pulled out the barbed grappling hook and knelt to wedge it over the threshold of the elevator door. When she was satisfied it wouldn't slip, she gripped the grapnel's handle and hopped into the shaft.

It was only a one-story trip, but the grapnel performed beautifully. The cord unspooled smoothly, allowing her to descend at a tolerable speed and land lightly on the concrete floor. She could have freehanded it, but sometimes, a girl wanted to travel in style.

She pressed a button on the gun, and the resulting *pop* told her the barbs on the hook had retracted. Ellis stepped aside as the hook clattered on the concrete, then reeled it in, stashed the grapnel, and inspected the doors leading to sub-basement three.

They weren't brushed steel like those on the floor above, and the gap between the doors was barely visible. Ellis got the jimmy out again and tried to insert it between the doors, but it slid away with a metallic *screech.*

She tried again, this time holding the jimmy perpendicular to the doors and pushing in with all her strength. *Nothing.*

Ellis thought about the hole Trissa had blasted through the roof of Charlie's car and wished for her shadow magic.

It can't hurt to try. That was a lie. It *did* hurt to try. Not physically, although the experience was reminiscent of banging her head against a brick wall. No, each attempt was a minute erosion of her confidence.

She reached for the corners of the elevator shaft, where the vague shapes dissolved into undifferentiated black. All she needed was a sliver of space between the doors.

A tendril of shadow magic brushed her fingertips, and Ellis could have cried with joy. She wanted to yank it close and capture it, but she forced herself to relax. She drew three deep breaths, then coaxed the fragile thread closer.

The magic inched up the steel, thinning as it went. Ellis pulled it with the delicacy of cotton candy until finally she flattened the magic into a blade and thrust it into the gap between the doors.

The line cracked open a hair.

Ellis whooped in celebration. The shout echoed up the cavernous elevator shaft, and she slapped a hand over her mouth.

She admired the visible divot in the machined metal. Had her magic returned? Feeling hopeful and relaxed by the familiar darkness, she grabbed for more shadows. She longed to feel the familiar shift of invisibility.

The magic dissipated under her eager efforts, and Ellis cursed. *Not back to full strength.*

She slipped the moonsteel jimmy into the new crack and pressed on the other end to lever the doors open. It required more pressure than it had for the doors on the level above, but eventually, the doors opened a quarter-inch, then a hand's width. Finally, Ellis could slip through the open foot of space. The doors stayed open behind her.

The hall beyond was disappointingly ordinary. It was a duplicate of the level above, with polished concrete floors and doors along the sides. The only unusual thing was a set of vents near the ceiling, about two feet wide and twenty inches high. Normally, metal grates covered vents of this sort, but these were open. Ellis peered into the nearest but saw nothing but aluminum inside.

Small, shiny objects were installed below the vents. They looked like fire alarms but were unmarked. Ellis couldn't determine their function. She shrugged and tried the handle of the nearest door, which was unlocked. She waited, listening for noises inside, and when she was reasonably certain it was deserted, she opened the door.

It was empty. No furniture, no boxes. Nothing. She hit the switch beside the door, but the overhead light fixture stayed dark.

What the hell was down here? Why would you install such heavy security on an empty basement?

The sign on the next door indicated that it was a stairway. Ellis felt resistance, a cotton-like ripping, as she pushed the door open. Some sticky, silky material stretched from the top of the door to the far wall, then slackened.

Ellis frowned and brushed the strands. Her fingers came away tacky with adhesive.

The strands of silk cast small rainbows in the fluorescent light from the hallway, but Ellis couldn't appreciate the beauty or process the revelation that there were even deeper levels under the Bromeliad because the staircase was filled with raw cave widow silk.

In Los Angeles, you joined the Marines if you had something to prove. In the Swallow's Nest, you became a silker. People trained for three years to harvest raw cave widow silk.

The silk wasn't dangerous, and it had healing properties. The infirmary used it to treat broken bones. The danger was the cave widows.

The spiders' venom didn't kill you. What fun would that be? The venom induced euphoric tranquility. You smiled and laughed while the spider ate you alive.

Something clicked in the darkest corner of the stairwell. Ellis' hand clenched around the shaft of the moonsteel jimmy.

There couldn't be a cave widow in this staircase. Cave widows lived underground. Sub-basement three *was* underground, but it was in a building. What would the spiders eat?

Intruders.

The shadows shifted, and Ellis saw that there was nothing in the corner. She exhaled a sigh of relief and glanced at the silk stretched across the doorway. Maybe it was Halloween decorations, or carpet fluff.

Behind the clinging white ropes of silk, a shape moved on the ceiling.

Click, click.

The hall light hit the spider's fist-sized eyes and shattered into dancing prisms as it crept toward Ellis on the threshold. She tried to close the steel door, but a rope of silk shot out of the spider's torso and held the door open. Ellis' muscles burned as she pulled, but cave widow silk was stronger than steel.

The spider gracefully leaped off the ceiling and landed near the door, then stuck several of its limbs into the gap.

Ellis ran. She took pleasure in running, in the swift movement and the air on her face. Now, she felt only fear and a desperate desire for more speed. Her feet slapped the concrete loudly enough to drown out the arachnid clicking along behind her.

Something moved in the space between the elevator doors. Was the elevator cage descending? No, the shape in the shaft was not metallic but organic. Another cave widow.

It pressed its mouth against the opening. On either side of its jaw, it had extra appendages called pedipalps lined with sharp barbs. Based on the size of its mouth, this spider was bigger than the one behind her.

It stretched two legs through the gap and stopped, too big to fit through the door. The portion of its abdomen that pressed against the gap was taut and black, and something was writhing within it. This was a brood mother ready to give birth.

Ellis shuddered and skidded to a halt. The only thing worse than fighting two cave widows would be fighting two hundred.

She glanced at the spider that had followed her from the staircase. It was moving cautiously, pincers tasting the air as it left a sticky trail. Its head moved rapidly, which gave the impression that it was looking at Ellis with every facet of its four compound eyes.

The spider reared and shot silk out of its torso toward Ellis. She dodged, and the white rope hit the ceiling above her head.

The spider skittered up the impromptu tightrope, then leaped. Small red dots on its underbelly caught the light. In other circumstances, they would have been beautiful.

Ellis dove and slid across the tile floor until she hit the trail of spider goo. It halted her in place and made it hard to regain her feet, which allowed the spider to leap on top of her. Its fangs glistened with the sedative that would turn her into a grinning dead woman.

Ellis kicked the monster in the face, and it sank its fangs into the sole of her boot. *This is why I don't wear sandals.*

The spider pushed away with a wild skittering of limbs on concrete, and its thrashing intensified when it realized it hadn't successfully bitten Ellis.

Ellis swung the moonsteel bar at the nearest limb, which snapped and dripped goo on Ellis' jeans. The spider flailed and pierced Ellis' side with another talon.

Another swing of the jimmy, and another snapped leg. Ellis kicked the cave widow's spotted torso hard enough to send it flying down the hall, leaving a fang embedded in her boot.

A metallic noise echoed through the hall. For a single, horrifying moment, Ellis thought the brood mother in the elevator shaft had shoved the doors open, but the rippling abdomen was still pressed against the gap. It wasn't the brood mother. The elevator was descending.

The small devices below the vents flashed red and emitted an uncanny noise, a barely audible twanging. The spider that had bitten Ellis paused, then skittered away on its remaining legs into the nearest vent.

The brood mother disappeared from the elevator doors just before the car slid into place. Ellis gripped her moon-steel bar and steeled herself for a different kind of fight.

The inner doors opened. Hector stood inside the elevator car.

Ellis sighed in relief, then hesitated when she saw he held a long knife.

The outer doors didn't move—Ellis had apparently broken the opening mechanism—but Hector managed to slip through the gap. His gaze traveled over the open vents and the blinking red lights, then landed on Ellis. He eyed the weapon in her hand, then the tear in her shirt.

Ellis tried to look relaxed. "Hey, Hector."

He finished his scan of the hallway, and when he was satisfied Ellis was alone, he sheathed his blade in a leather scabbard. "You shouldn't be here."

A needle of pain spiked between Ellis' eyes as she stood. Her adrenaline was crashing. "That's an understatement."

MARTHA CARR & MICHAEL ANDERLE

He gripped her arm a little too hard and guided her toward the elevator door. He had to release her arm to squeeze into the elevator, but after he entered, he watched her and waited as though he expected her to run. She followed him in, eager to get away from the spiders, and Hector hit the button for the third floor. Ellis was on edge, so the elevator ride took an eternity.

The spiders had disappeared when they saw the red lights and heard the twanging tone, and both had turned off when the elevator arrived. Someone had trained them to guard sub-basement three. How was that possible? Cave widows weren't domesticated, for one, and she had no idea why cave widows would be in the basement of a Los Angeles social club.

On the third floor, Hector took Ellis to his office. For someone with access to a woman as powerful as Amelia, the office seemed small and drab. The desk and chair were functional, and the only decorations were a set of movie posters for old 1920s horror movies, including, Ellis noted with a wry smile, *Nosferatu*.

Hector started making tea using an electric kettle he kept on a file cabinet. "Glad I still have tea. I hardly spend any time here. Amelia offered me a bigger space, but I told her the whole building was my office."

"Does that include sub-basement three?" They would have to talk about it eventually, and Ellis wanted to put him on the defensive.

Hector shook his head. "That's out of my domain."

Ellis perched on a folding chair. "How did you get in?"

He was frustratingly relaxed. "I stole a spare key from

the secret compartment in Amelia's desk she doesn't think I know about."

"That's dangerous."

Hector's fingers brushed the hilt of his knife. "Amelia told me if I ever went down there, I should bring a knife. Obviously, she was drunk. It was an empty hallway."

If only you knew. "I meant stealing from Amelia."

Hector snickered. Ellis was suddenly sad that he hadn't seen the cave widows. He would have appreciated the giant spiders, albeit briefly before they ate him.

"What did you expect to find down there?" she asked.

Hector shrugged. "I'm not sure. Booby traps? Lava? Snake pits?"

"I found a staircase to a lower level. Maybe the snake pits are down there."

Hector grimaced. He was clearly unwilling to intrude further on Amelia's territory. "It doesn't matter. I probably shouldn't have gone down there, and you *definitely* shouldn't have. Did you climb down the shaft?"

Ellis decided not to extol the virtues of her new grapnel. "Yeah."

"Why?" He was serious. If he didn't like her answer, she suspected he would tell Amelia.

Ellis imagined explaining the complicated situation to Hector. *I went down there because Amelia wears a ring with the symbol of a secret society my dead mother's connected to, and I hate secrets.* No, that would *not* fly.

She raced through increasingly implausible explanations and was on, "I was sleepwalking," when an idea came to her. "I was looking for room to expand our mushroom grow-op."

Hector's eyebrows shot up. "What? In sub-basement *three*?"

"I thought improved climate control might prevent further nightmare nodes. Temperature becomes more consistent the deeper you go. It's easier to manage."

"Uh-huh."

She could tell he didn't believe her, but what she had said might be true, and Hector wanted to believe her more than he wanted the truth.

"Aside from the nodes, we're doing well," she continued. "We should start thinking about expansion. Amelia encourages entrepreneurial spirit."

Hector was still uneasily eyeing the puncture wound in her side. Ellis adjusted her shirt to cover herself. "I'd love to tell you what I have in mind." She let a smile cross her face. "Let me take you out. Think of it as an apology for breaking your elevator doors."

Hector's answering smile was so genuine it hurt, although her gratitude wasn't a ruse. She didn't know how the fight would have gone if Hector hadn't triggered the alarms.

She pointed at his scabbard. "Do you know how to use that?" His posture suggested that he did, but a short sword wasn't the typical weapon of choice for a twenty-first-century man.

Hector smiled enigmatically. "I do. Take me somewhere nice, and I'll tell you about it."

A jolt of pleasure shot up Ellis' spine. "You've got yourself a deal. Only…"

He raised an eyebrow.

"You won't tell Amelia I was down there, will you?" She put on a sweet, nervous smile.

"Not if you won't tell her I copied her elevator key."

He copied *it?* Ellis' smile turned genuine. This would be fun.

CHAPTER NINE

Liza Laponte grimaced at her half-eaten breakfast. The bacon was already cold.

Her server paused by her table. "Is the food okay, hon? We got a new line cook back there, so if the eggs are wrong…"

"The eggs are fine." She didn't actually know. She hadn't touched them. "I'm just not hungry today. Can I get another coffee? To go?" She drained the last of her ceramic mug.

The server murmured an agreement and bustled away.

Liza sighed. She hadn't slept well since her conversation with Morrissey. In truth, she hadn't gotten a full eight hours since he'd started talking about the "mysterious vigilante" stalking the rooftops of Los Angeles.

The server dropped off her bill and her to-go coffee. Liza left a twenty-percent tip down to the cent. She always tipped well here, which meant she received good service. Liza treated people fairly, and she expected fair treatment in return. That could be a strength or a weakness.

She was treating Charlie fairly, and he was being an asshole. He had erected walls that hobbled their long and productive collaboration. It pissed her off.

Liza had once thought they might become romantically involved. It would have made sense. They were the same age, in good shape, and had similar interests. More importantly, they understood each other. Homicide detective work was interpersonally challenging and emotional, and a lover who understood that would be valuable.

Now, even their friendship was on thin ice.

She suspected Charlie was lying about the new captain. It was *possible* that Irving was among the many sexist jerks she'd encountered in her career, but Charlie had been *trying* to get under her skin.

She would make her own threat assessment of the captain. If Irving was a problem, she would face it head-on. She suddenly wanted to rifle through her desk drawer, find her commendations, and pin them on her blazer.

Liza sighed. A bad boss wouldn't care about medals, and a good boss would already know, so she went to Montgomery Irving's office empty-chested. The door was closed, and she peered through the glass. No one was inside, so she knocked.

She heard the shuffle of feet on wood, and the door opened.

"Hello, Captain. I'm—"

"Liza Laponte," he cut in. "Come in, Detective."

He stepped into her personal space. Liza briefly wondered if this visit had been a mistake, but he merely closed the door behind her. It was weird, but not in the way Liza was worried about.

She stood straight-backed in front of the desk until he waved her to a chair. Then she eyed the bare walls. Irving's interior design communicated austerity.

He sat. "Everything all right with the Sanders case?"

Liza blinked. Irving was well-informed. Randolph Sanders was a drive-by shooting victim. Liza was the lead detective on his case, working alongside the gang unit.

"We haven't caught him, sir. Amazing how a man can be shot at a barbecue in broad daylight, and no one sees anything." The neighborhood had clammed up.

Irving nodded. "It's frustrating. Build relationships. They'll come in handy on the next case, if not this one. Let me know if you need additional resources. Is that why you came?"

"No, sir." Liza shifted uncomfortably. So far, she liked Irving, but she had to navigate these unfamiliar waters carefully. "I wanted to float an idea." Irving remained pleasant. "About switching partners."

His eyebrows drew together. "Oh. I was under the impression…"

"Sir?"

"You and Morrissey are a highly effective team. You have a clearance rate almost as high as Ron Jackson's." There was a grim question in that. *Was Charlie Morrissey involved in dirty business too?*

"I'm not asking you to rat anyone out," he added. "I want to understand the landscape. I'd like to excise Ron Jackson's rot without killing the host."

Liza understood. Ron Jackson had been fired, but plenty of his cronies hadn't. Removing everyone who was even *lightly* infected with his decay would destroy the department.

"Charlie…er, Detective Morrissey wasn't mixed up with Ron. I'd say they were enemies, honestly."

"Enemies, as in competitors?"

"No. Morrissey wasn't horning in on Ron's dirty business. I don't think so, anyway."

"Ah." The syllable hung between them.

Irving had monumental patience, but finally, he asked, "Then why the switch request? What do you suspect?"

It was a great question, and one she had asked herself. What *was* Charlie up to? What was the deal with his busted car, his trips to that downtown apartment complex, and all the times he'd lied about where he was going? If he was married, she'd suspect an affair. If he had a girlfriend, he would have told Liza, if only to keep things between them as clear as glacial Alaskan waters.

Irving's placidity wouldn't last forever. Liza had to make a choice.

"Something weird is happening." She pulled up the image of the purple woman on her phone and showed it to Irving.

Irving brought the phone close to his face and twitched a pair of reading glasses onto his nose. His expression was not disbelieving but intent. "Tell me about this image."

The question was so open-ended that it would make an agoraphobe nervous. Liza had wanted an emotional signal from the captain that would tell her how to proceed, but he had chucked the ball back into her court.

"I'm not saying I believe in aliens, sir, but I don't know what to make of this."

"Doctored?"

"Digital Forensics says no."

"Technology these days…"

Liza walked him through the steps she'd taken to verify the photograph, and he pursed his lips. "Plus," she finished, "the top was blown off Morrissey's car."

"Blown off? How?"

"Obliterated. There's a big hole in it that wasn't there before. And…" Her voice trailed off. This was where she could get into trouble.

"Yes?"

"I know he was up in Topanga the day this photo was taken."

"Oh?"

"I followed him."

That elicited no reaction beyond a nod. "If your relationship has deteriorated to the point where you're staking out your partner, you shouldn't be working together."

She couldn't tell if he was scolding her. The man was unreadable. He might transfer her back to Vice, or hell, to the traffic squad. Liza Laponte, LA's most decorated meter maid.

"Do you believe in the supernatural, Detective?"

Liza blinked. "My grandfather saw a ghost once, sir."

"That's not an answer."

"He was the most honest man I've ever known."

"So, you believed him?"

"I believe in evidence, Captain. It's what makes me a good detective." *A decorated detective.* "I had eyewitness testimony."

A smile appeared on Irving's lips. "How much time do

you have left on your shift? If you're up for it, I have a special project for you."

"Color me curious."

"I think you'll like it."

He left her to consider the cryptic comment and punched a memorized number into his phone. "I'm bringing someone. Send a car," he told the person on the other end of the call.

What was she signing up for? He offered no further explanation, and Liza asked no additional questions since she already felt like she was on thin ice. Maybe he was working with the FBI or the NSA. The acronym agencies sometimes operated in Los Angeles.

Her curiosity grew when a black van was waiting for them in the parking garage. The dark tint on the windows made it impossible to see the faces of anyone inside, but there were clearly two people in the front seat. She guessed they were male from their builds.

The door on the side of the van popped open with a pneumatic hiss, and for the first time, Liza hesitated.

"I'll see you tomorrow," Irving assured her. "You'll know more by then."

Liza relaxed. You didn't set meetings with people you were about to drop into the Mariana Trench wearing cement pumps.

"Have fun," the captain added as Liza stepped into the van. The door closed. There was a metal grate between her and the drivers.

Liza realized that Captain Irving had not returned her phone.

CHAPTER TEN

Take me somewhere nice, Hector had said. Ellis picked at the black lace hem of her dress and hoped the rooftop tiki bar qualified.

Mama Shelter perched on top of a hotel in Hollywood, and it served up fruit-forward cocktails and terrific views of downtown Los Angeles. The bar occupied half the rooftop. The other half featured a small pool surrounded by lounge chairs.

Ellis decided she wanted to spend her next day off here in a swimsuit, drinking rum spiked with pineapple juice. If she was lucky, that would be three or four years from now.

Her new dress seemed funereal compared to the palm fronds and umbrella drinks. She had several little black dresses, but she'd bought a new one for tonight, shorter and tighter than her norm. She'd also bought low pumps with chunky heels she hoped would be moderately effective at kicking someone's face in if things went south.

She had chosen the tiny dress as an offensive weapon

against Hector's inevitable questions. It was a distraction to make him forget the basement.

She wished *she* could forget the basement. The memory gave her goosebumps.

The tight black fabric rubbed the puncture in her side. She'd treated it with a mushroom ointment, but it wouldn't heal for another few days.

Hector slid a tall pink drink in front of her. "Are you all right?"

She grabbed the glass. "I will be after I drink this." It was cold, and the mint garnish smelled wonderful.

Hector was about to ask her a question. She could feel it in her bones. To head him off, she slurped her straw. "I hope this place is fancy enough."

Hector grinned and lifted his pinkie finger off his glass, which was as blue as hers was pink. Ellis didn't understand the gesture, but he was smiling, so she mirrored him. He raised his chin and looked down his nose at her, and she slurped aggressively in response.

"I could go for tacos," she remarked.

Hector hummed agreeably. "There's a tapas place in Los Feliz that does a terrific charred octopus tostada, and the tableside guac is phenomenal. Should we change venues?"

Ellis didn't want sixteen dollars' worth of charred octopus that she could eat in one bite. She wanted *truck* tacos from a parking lot. Or a strip mall. Or outside a dive bar.

"Maybe later," Ellis replied. "I'm still deciding whether I want to take a dip in the pool."

Hector cleared his throat. The questioning look was

back. Ellis aimed her dress' plunging neckline at him, but it was no use.

"Are you planning to tell me why you were in the basement?" he asked.

Ellis stared longingly at the bright turquoise rectangle on the other side of the roof. If she threw herself in, Hector would chivalrously fish her out, find her a towel, offer her his coat, and return to asking annoying questions.

What answer would he accept? What answer would anyone in LA accept for her ridiculous behavior?

Ellis drew a deep breath, then demurely sipped her cocktail and tried not to look pathetic as she announced, "I need money."

"You thought Amelia kept some in the basement?" He eyed her skeptically. She wished she had worn a cheaper dress.

"I wasn't trying to steal anything." *Although I might reconsider if there's anything valuable down there.* "My brother is sick, and his medications are expensive. I was being entrepreneurial."

In Ellis' experience, sick relatives were a go-to excuse for criminal behavior in American movies and TV shows.

Hector winced. "I'm so sorry. What's wrong?"

Landon's grinning lilac face flashed through her mind. *He has terminal asshole-itis.* "He has a skin condition." She gazed across the skyline with an expression she hoped would discourage further questioning.

Hector put his hand over hers. His fingertips were rough, and his touch sent pinpricks of pleasure up her arm. They dissipated under her guilt over the deep concern on his face.

She didn't move her hand. "Thank you. It's been challenging. The mushroom grow-op has been going well, so I thought if I brought a few new strains into the mix, I could make more money. Since we've just about maxed out sub-basement two with the sterile room and substrate storage..."

"You could have asked me for help."

"I didn't want to make a fuss until I could find space. I wanted to do the legwork. I was looking for opportunities, not charity."

He nodded in understanding. "New mushroom varietals, huh? You still haven't told me where you get them. I have half a mind to contact a mycologist. UCLA probably has one."

"No!" Ellis blurted, then added, "Amelia would be furious if she lost her monopoly."

"That's true." Hector was uneasy. He was as afraid of Amelia as Ellis was. She and Hector had not being stupid in common. "Where did you learn, anyway?"

"The mushroom stuff, or the breaking and entering?"

He snorted. "Both."

"Family business. The mushrooms, that is." A wave of homesickness for the drow caverns washed over her. They were so unlike this open rooftop. "I didn't know my mom, but my dad's big into mushrooms. What do your parents think of your monsters?"

Hector chuckled. "My mom hates horror since she's a scaredy-cat, but she's incredibly supportive. When I show her something spooky I've been working on, she drinks a big glass of wine first and holds my dad's hand."

His face dimmed. "They're more proud of me for

working at the Bromeliad than they are for anything I care about."

Ellis frowned. "You don't care about the Bromeliad? This from the man who's regularly there at five in the morning to handle mushroom shipments?"

Hector rolled his eyes. "I *care*, but it's not the same. My parents view 'special effects artist to facilities manager' as a successful career progression. It's not an unusual story, mind you. People abandon their dreams all the time in this town."

She didn't like seeing him morose. Ellis wished she could show him the spiders, although it might remind him of those abandoned dreams.

In the absence of spiders, she leaned over and kissed him. When their lips brushed, her elbow slipped and knocked over his tall drink.

Ellis yelped and scooted away from the flood of blue curaçao. Hector wasn't as lucky. Vibrant blue soaked his cream-colored pants.

"Shit!" He leaped off his stool and dabbed the spreading stain with a napkin. He was annoyed, although he was trying not to show it.

"I'm *so* sorry." She offered him another napkin.

"Never apologize for kissing me." He ran a hand through his hand and flashed her a wan smile, and the chill went down a degree. "I'd better find a sink."

He disappeared into the building. Ellis gazed into the beautiful turquoise water of the pool. She didn't think she'd try kissing him again. Not tonight, anyway.

CHAPTER ELEVEN

Ellis stood over a tray of rustcaps and scowled at her humidity meter. If she couldn't control this, the nightmare nodes would come back if they hadn't already. For the umpteenth time, she poked the growth matrix beneath the mushrooms to test for nodules. There was nothing but wet mulch.

She didn't look up when Hector came in, although she straightened in surprise when he laid a hand on her back. It was warm through her thin T-shirt.

"I brought you a present," Hector announced. He held up a container in a grocery bag.

She brightened. "Ooh, is that the new nutrient mix from those mushroom people on TikTok? We can try it with the next batch of rustcaps."

He laughed. "No, it's chicken soup."

Ellis cocked her head. "I'm not sure we can feed the mushrooms chicken soup, but we can start a test tray if you want."

Hector snorted. "The soup isn't for the mushrooms. It's

for you. For your brother, actually. I made the bone broth from scratch. I'll have an even better batch in a few days."

Ellis felt as dirty as her fingernails. "Oh."

He blushed. "I know it won't solve your brother's problems. Chicken soup can't fix everything, but it makes me feel better, and I have an inkling that you're not much of a cook."

"I could cook! Probably. If I tried."

He stashed the soup in their work fridge while providing insultingly detailed directions about how to reheat it.

"I can *reheat soup!*"

His eyes sparkled. "That's the positive attitude you'll want to maintain when you pour the soup into a saucepan and set the burner to low."

He didn't mention the kiss they'd shared, if it even qualified as a kiss. *Our lips bumped together.* How many seconds did it have to last before it counted?

"I have another gift," Hector added.

Ellis smiled. "Landon will be thrilled."

"This one's for you." He pressed a key into her hand.

Ellis stared at the object in the dim light. "Is this the key for the sub-basement?"

"Sure is. I made another copy."

Ellis bounced on the balls of her feet. Hector grinned, but his hesitation lingered. "I guess the key to a woman's heart is illicit access to sub-basement three."

"The key to *this* woman's heart is," she eagerly replied.

Charlie would have tried to stop me. At least, he would have told me not to go.

Ellis wrapped her arms around Hector's neck and

leaned in, determined to "bump lips" until it counted. Hector hesitated, then relaxed into the kiss. His arms slipped around her waist.

After what felt like forever but not long enough, Ellis pulled away. She couldn't afford more distractions from her mission, but the absence of his lips saddened her.

"Did you bring your sword?" she asked.

He blinked. "My *what?*"

"Your sword. The sword you were carrying yesterday when you re…"

She paused. Was "rescued" the right word? It made her sound like a damsel in distress. "When you thwarted my basement adventure."

Hector grinned. "Oh, that's a *kodachi*. I practice *tankendo* a few times a week. We use wooden swords in class, though. I've never fought with a sharp blade."

"Do you think you could?" She needed to know, but she couldn't let on why.

Fortunately, Hector took the question seriously and nodded after some thought. "If I needed to, I could."

"Great. In that case, when are we going back down?"

"Tonight, if you're willing. I'd say now, but we should wait for less foot traffic."

"In other words, we should wait for Amelia to leave."

"The night watchman owes me a favor, so if there's any trouble, it won't spread."

"Sounds like a plan."

CHAPTER TWELVE

The day dragged on. Ellis had plenty of work to do, but she resented the lack of excitement involved in tending mushrooms.

Amelia came down to check on them. Ellis panicked, certain their boss would dig through her pockets, find the elevator key, and...

She wasn't sure how the woman would react. The Bromeliad's owner had a unique flavor of menace. Mob bosses probably owed her favors.

If she catches you in sub-basement three, you'll never leave. The thought stuck in Ellis' mind and tempered her anticipation.

They left at six with a promise to return later that evening.

At her apartment, Ellis cleaned her new grapnel, then attached a small bag of dried firecap powder to it.

"You planning something, girlie?" Percy was wearing lemon-yellow pajamas covered in psychedelic swirls. With

Muffler wrapped around his neck and Wormy perched on his shoulder, he resembled St. Francis on acid.

Ellis filled him in on Hector and the Bromeliad's basement, although she left out the cave widows. She also omitted the kiss.

"Have you ever talked to a spider?" she inquired.

"As much as I've talked to any insect. Their brains aren't wired for language. Most animals' brains aren't, o' course, but dogs can get the hang of it."

Flower insinuated herself under Ellis' hand on cue, and Ellis petted the pit bull's silky back. Her short tail wagged enthusiastically.

"Why do you wanna know about our arachnid friends?"

Ellis hoped she'd never be so unlucky as to have a cave widow *friend*. Also, telling Percy about cave widows would bring him closer to the truth about the drow, and she wasn't ready for that.

"There were spiders in the basement." It was an understatement, but Percy didn't comment.

Ellis removed a dagger from her underwear drawer and inspected the blade. It was well-made, but it wasn't moonsteel, and it was too short. When she could stab a cave widow with it, she'd be within range of its talons and fangs.

She searched the stacked pallets in her walk-in closet until she found a hand rake with three sharp points and decided that while she was in there, she might as well test her shadow magic.

She slid the door shut and turned off the dim lights. The door was hermetically sealed, so she was in complete darkness.

Magic pulsed in the shadows. Her sense of it was weak, as though thick gauze covered her hands, but it was there.

Ellis reached for it, but the darkness shied away and dissolved at her touch. She needed to relax, but her desperation increased as she destroyed the magic she touched.

She clenched her teeth and gripped a tendril of shadow. It wriggled in her fingers for a second, then shattered, and her hand closed on nothing.

Ellis sighed. She couldn't rely on it.

She flung the closet door open and winced at the bright bedroom light.

"Do you still have that soldering iron, Percy?" she called.

The pet psychic skipped in, aglow with cheerful anticipation. His main problem these days was boredom, aside from the widespread manhunt targeting him. He was eager to help, no matter what the project.

An hour later, she drove back to the Bromeliad with a makeshift trident on her back. Using a soldering iron, super glue, leather cord, and most of a roll of duct tape, they'd replaced the rake's handgrip with a broom handle. She looked like an extremely aggressive gardener.

She'd eaten a bowl of Hector's chicken soup for dinner. It was tasty, and his thoughtfulness warmed her spirits. She was in an excellent mood when she raced into sub-basement two.

Unfortunately, she forgot about the long pole strapped to her back. The top caught the lintel, and her feet flew out from under her.

Hector made a noble effort not to laugh as he helped

her to her feet, then unclipped the trident from her back and inspected the soldered joints.

"Don't give me that look," Ellis defensively said.

"I'm not giving you any look," he protested. "I don't know many women with soldering irons, that's all."

He ran his hand along the broom handle, then touched the prongs of the rake. She'd sharpened them. He raised an eyebrow. "I'm glad you're prepared to assess the basement's suitability for additional grow space." He obviously, and correctly, suspected there was more to this venture than she'd disclosed.

Ellis praised the scabbard hanging from his waist, then unsnapped the leather strap that held the blade in. If he had to use it, every second would count.

For the first time, she detected anxiety in his gaze. She got a whiff of his cologne and took the trident back before the scent distracted her. "Ready?"

His hand settled on the hilt of his *kodachi.* "Time to assess the forbidden basement for mushroom-farming suitability."

Ellis smothered her laugh behind tight lips and gripped the trident tighter.

They entered the elevator side-by-side. When Hector turned the key in the lock, Ellis held her breath. Surely, it would set off an alarm, or Amelia would be there, or a cave widow would drop from a ceiling hatch.

Nothing happened. When the doors opened on sub-basement three, familiar red lights flashed, and the twanging tone played through hidden loudspeakers. Ellis watched the dark mouths of the uncovered vents, but nothing moved. The well-trained spiders stayed hidden.

Ellis and Hector advanced to the door that would permit them entry into the bowels of the Bromeliad. "Ready for advanced mushroom farming?" Ellis asked, and when Hector nodded, she pushed it open.

The staircase had more open vents. She hadn't noticed them the first time, and she wondered where they led. Was there a vault full of webs crawling with hungry spiders and pulsing with glistening egg sacs? She hoped she'd never find out.

The descent was quick. Ellis was relieved to discover there was only one level below sub-basement three. The thought of an infinitely descending staircase creeped her out.

Other than the prospect of cave widows, there was nothing frightening about the unadorned concrete and metal stairwell. Still, Ellis jumped at every echoing footstep, and her mind invented skittering arachnid shapes in the shadows.

The door at the bottom of the stairs was clay-colored particleboard, and a window stretched along one side. Ellis peered through the plexiglass. The corridor beyond was blurred and featureless.

She put her ear against the door and picked up faint footsteps on the other side. They were coming this way.

Ellis whispered, "Get back!" and pushed Hector away from the window. The air in the staircase suddenly felt thick and oppressive. She didn't want to meet whoever was approaching.

There was a gap under the staircase, a triangle of space that wouldn't be visible to anyone who opened the door. Ellis chivvied Hector in, then squeezed against him just before the door opened.

"Eight years in the Marines, and now I carry sacks of dead rats," a man muttered. Something soft bumped and dragged on the stairs. Hector's hand drifted to his sword, but he stayed silent.

A woman replied, "If you'd like to volunteer, I'm sure they'd prefer live prey."

"I heard the boss brings 'em live gerbils sometimes. He likes to watch them hunt." The man's tone was light, as though he were discussing juicy office gossip, not juicy gerbils.

"I heard he collects feral cats," the woman grimly added. "Enough that Animal Control has noticed."

The rustle of equipment suggested they were both carrying guns. Overkill for cave widows, but she couldn't blame them, especially if it was feeding time.

She thought they were soldiers based on their equipment and clipped conversational style, but that confused her. Ellis had spent enough time at the Bromeliad to notice special ops forces regularly disappearing into the elevators.

In under a minute, the two soldiers went through the door at the top of the stairs, and Ellis realized with a start that she was so close to Hector that she was spooning him. It wasn't unpleasant, although she *had* hoped it would happen on a sofa, or at least a thick carpet, rather than under a staircase, cowering from spider-chow-distributing commandos. At least it was warm.

"What do they mean, 'live prey?'" True to Hector's nature, he sounded excited, although he was alarmed.

As though in answer, the level above exploded into high-pitched shrieking and the clicking of talons on concrete. It sounded like a screaming hailstorm.

"What the fuck is that?" he hissed.

"The reason Amelia told you to bring a knife," Ellis whispered back. "It'll be okay. We just have to wait."

The noise soon abated, and the soldiers returned. This time, they were silent. Ellis doubted feeding cave widows was enjoyable. When the door closed behind them, Ellis and Hector crawled out from under the staircase.

Ellis listened at the door, then looked at her companion. "Still game to check it out?"

"I'm in over my head here, but…" He greedily gazed at the door.

"You're curious."

"Sure am."

"In that case, gentlemen first!" she exclaimed.

Hector drew a deep breath, opened the door, and stepped inside. He immediately paused and muttered, "What the hell?"

Ellis slipped in beside him and gasped.

The door opened onto a featureless fifty-foot-long hallway. The space in front of the door was clear, but beyond that, glittering lightsilk threads hung from the ceiling. They were stapled to the drywall and spaced scant inches apart.

The strings obscured their view of the end of the hall, but Ellis thought it turned sharply to the right. If there were any doors between here and there, she couldn't see them.

The wall at the end of the corridor was decorated with an insignia composed of sharp black lines, a visual break in the endless beige. The streaming silk strands blurred it, but Ellis was certain it depicted a half-moon inside two concentric circles.

Ellis instinctively backed away from the dense curtain of lightsilk.

Hector reached for the nearest thread. "What *is* this?"

Ellis blurted, "Don't!" but he had touched it.

"Is it an art installation?" Hector plunged his hand into the silk.

Ellis shuddered. "We have to leave."

He turned, and strands of lightsilk slid through his fingers like water. A few slipped off his hand and rippled into the rest. It would have been beautiful if it wasn't terrifying.

She remembered how the lightsilk confetti had burned, and she cringed away from the fluttering silk threads. It probably looked like she was cringing away from Hector.

"Ellis?" He reached for her, but a strand of lightsilk dangled from his fingers.

Ellis brought her trident up between them. "Stop!"

He froze and frowned. "Are you okay?"

"No. I want to go." Her voice cracked. "You first." She nudged him with the trident.

"Okay. I'm going."

She waited until he was in the hallway before leaving the corner into which she'd tucked herself. The lightsilk was still swaying, and she had to wait for it to settle before she could yank open the door and rush through.

The cave widows had been a clue, and the lightsilk confirmed it. Whoever had designed this basement was deeply familiar with drow and was actively defending their operation against them.

Ellis was upset and wanted to run, but she was afraid to touch Hector. She would have to inspect his clothing to ensure that none of the lightsilk had stuck to him.

The memory of the confetti consumed her. It had felt like red-hot ball bearings puncturing every part of her, and it had drained her magic, which was worse. She missed her shadow magic.

She couldn't risk traversing that burning forest, but what lay past the half-moon symbol? Someone had gone to incredible lengths to protect it from her.

Maybe it was self-aggrandizing to think they'd had her in mind.

Ellis' nerves sang on the way back to the elevator. She hoped a cave widow would attack her. She wanted to use her new trident, but more than that, she wanted a good fight to turn her fear into focus.

The empty black vents mocked her.

The elevator machinery whirred, the floor vibrated beneath them, and Ellis sighed. "I don't think we should expand into sub-basement four."

"No," Hector agreed. "Although those hanging threads were pretty."

She didn't respond.

CHAPTER THIRTEEN

The abortive trip had lasted less than an hour. The empty late-night streets hastened her ride home, and soon, she slunk into her apartment with her untested trident.

Percy looked up from his computer in surprise. "Back so soon?"

Ellis groaned. "I hit a wall. Well, sort of. I hit a hallway."

He squinted. "How can you *hit* a hallway?"

"It's hard to explain." She threw herself on the sofa. "Do we have any food?"

Quiet animal noises filled the apartment. A handful of songbirds had taken over a hat rack in the corner. They ate birdseed from a feeder, hopped on the wooden poles, and kept an eye on the thin gray cat that was tracking their movements from across the room.

Muffler the ferret skittered onto the sofa and curled around Ellis' neck. Flower emerged from the kitchen with something gripped in her teeth, which she deposited in Ellis' lap. It was an energy bar.

Ellis gingerly picked it up and wiped off the dog slobber

on her jeans. Flower sniffed and looked away but relented under Ellis' head-pats.

"I don't think you were meant for the restaurant industry," Ellis told her.

The energy bar proudly announced its macronutrient and vitamin content in bold silver letters. Smaller gold letters identified the flavor as "muscle fuel."

Ellis pursed her lips. "Is there any *real* food?"

"We have no groceries, and I'm sick of takeout," Percy replied tartly. "If I have to eat one more bowl of sesame noodles, I will lose my mind. Those bars have every vital nutrient you need, so unless you care to hop down to the grocery store, don't complain."

Percy was generally cheerful, but today, he was slumped behind his computer with a thick worry line between his eyebrows, typing far slower than usual.

Ellis frowned. "Are you okay?"

He threw her a dark look. "I'm a homebody, Ellis, not a house-arrest-body. Man was not meant to live in a cage. Did you know there's a type of torture where they put you in an all-white room and don't let you see anyone?"

"Thanks to your pets, my walls *aren't* white. They're a grimy ombré."

Percy didn't pick up on the sarcasm. "That's true. I do appreciate the animals. They're good people." He scratched behind the rangy gray cat's ears. It had abandoned the birds in favor of curling up beside Percy. It started purring but stopped when it realized Ellis was looking and returned its face to an appropriately predatory expression.

"You've got cabin fever," Ellis stated.

"I don't know. Maybe."

"It wasn't a question."

Ellis was familiar with cabin fever. She'd experienced eighteen years of it before she'd first left the drow homestead. She could still remember the shocking gentle warmth of the sun on her skin as she hiked through the woods, though it had only been a few minutes.

Her father had disappeared without a word when he'd discovered her hiding under her blankets with a ferocious sunburn. She'd thought he was furious and he would inform the drow elders, but he returned an hour later with a fresh mushroom salve. He'd taught her how to make it herself, along with a lotion that would protect her from UV rays.

She'd thought that meant he wanted her to leave. She wasn't sure anymore.

Ellis shook the memory away. "You need an activity."

"I can fetch the backgammon board."

"Not a game. A task. Could you train an animal for a reconnaissance mission?"

The suggestion shocked him out of his lethargy. "Train? *Train?* I can *ask*. A *collaboration* would be possible if they're up for it, but I'm not a whip-wielding 'lion tamer.' It's up to my friends if they want to participate. What did you have in mind?"

Ellis sat cross-legged beside Percy, vibrating with anticipation. "So, there's this basement…"

She told him about the lightsilk threads dangling from the ceiling. She didn't tell him about the cave widows in case he took the spiders' side and also because he'd never send his animals into danger. Ellis told herself she'd protect them, but she couldn't get into the basement without their help.

"This might be a good job for the rats," Ellis suggested. "They're smart and scrappy, and they wouldn't seem out-of-place in a basement."

Muffler sniffed derisively on Ellis' shoulder, and she scratched him. "You can go too if you want, Muffy." The ferret squealed.

Percy hummed. "I can organize a mission, but I won't send the animals on their own. I gotta go with them."

"You'll be with them in spirit?" It sounded lame, even to her.

"Nice try. You promised me an activity."

"You can participate from here! It'll be active. You'll be actively watching a bunch of rats invade a basement."

He crossed his arms, and the divot between his eyebrows deepened.

"It's too dangerous, Percy!" she protested. "You're a fugitive! You can't go into a basement with one exit."

"Getting *in* is easy. I acknowledge that getting *out* might be a *skosh* more challenging."

Ellis groaned. She had already gotten Percy into so much trouble. She didn't think she could live with herself if he went to prison.

"I can barely use my powers. If you go to jail, I won't be able to spring you."

"That's my risk to take."

Ellis wondered whether Landon could pull off a jail-break, but his shadow magic was inconsistent. Not to mention that, unlike Ellis, he'd have limited time to work since he'd have to wear the medallion.

The medallion.

The medallion had turned Landon, Connor, and Trissa into a goofy brown-haired man. Would it do the same for Percy?

"I have an idea," Ellis said. "I think I know how you can safely go with the animals, but I'll have to confirm it. Will you start training them in the meantime? Please?"

Percy sighed. "S'pose so, but I'm serious, Ellis. Where they go, I go."

"Understood." Ellis barely listened as she texted Landon.

We need to meet.

She was antsy after sending the text, ready to leap into action, but Landon didn't have service in the homestead. It could be days before he received her message.

Ellis grabbed a purple composition book off the dining room table and tore out a page, which she handed to Percy.

"What's this for?" he asked.

"Make a grocery list. I'm going shopping."

CHAPTER FOURTEEN

Ellis spent the next twenty-four hours stocking the refrigerator with actual food and valiantly deploying a bottle of bleach to return her walls to their original snowy white. Her phone beeped while she was eating a plate of excellent vegan lasagna that a grateful Percy had assembled that afternoon.

Meet me in Valley Village Park tomorrow at noon. Wear a robe.

Ellis frowned. The location was straightforward. It was a greenspace along Highway 170 in North Hollywood. Ellis stared at the second half of the text for a full minute. A *robe?* What kind of robe? She didn't own a robe. Who owned a robe?

"*Percy!* I need to raid your closet!"

The purple silk kimono was *not* good motorcycle wear, but the park had no place to change, so the gown flapped under her leather jacket and over her black jeans. She felt conspicuous, but no one in the parking lot noticed. They were too busy wrangling children or checking out their friends' designer yoga pants.

It was a warm, clear, beautiful day. Ellis saw no sign of her brother as she left the parking lot and scanned her surroundings for anyone in a robe. The only person who vaguely matched that description was a tall woman with jet-black hair in a tight bun. Her robe was a red velvet cloak with an embroidered hem and a luxurious hood. Good enough.

The red velvet made the woman easy to follow as she strode toward a crowd in the distance. Several people at a picnic table waved enthusiastically, and the woman raised a wooden staff above her head in reply.

Ellis frowned. The staff was covered with foam padding. It would not be an effective weapon.

Ellis' suspicion that she had dramatically misinterpreted "robe" increased as she approached the assembled crowd. They wore a wide variety of tunics, chainmail, and leather bodices under thick wool cloaks, and they carried a multitude of weapons, although few had real blades.

A broad, tall man with hands as big as cave widows clapped Ellis on the shoulder. "You must be new, lass! We don't often see new folks. Welcome!"

Her shoulders nervously rose to her ears. "Um, I'm looking for my brother. Do you know anyone named Landon?"

"The elf?"

"What?"

Ellis panicked. What was happening? Had these people captured Landon? Worse, had he *told* them? She frantically searched for the half-moon symbol on the crowd's clothing and weapons. Had she fallen into a trap?

Landon emerged from between two young women who were stringing bows and comparing foam-tipped arrows and interrupted her freakout with a grin. "You made it!"

Ellis gaped. She had assumed Landon would be wearing his gold medallion, but he was one hundred percent drow: purple skin, white hair, and pointed ears on proud display.

She managed to collect her jaw from the lawn but remained speechless.

The imposing man was nonchalant about Landon's appearance. He mirrored her brother's grin. "Impressive, huh? Most people only do full-body makeup for Comic-Con or big LARP weekends, but Landon's committed. It must take hours. I don't know when he sleeps."

Landon shrugged. "It's not so hard once you get used to it."

Ellis squinted. There was something wrong with Landon's ears. Had he tried to make them look rounder? No, they still ended in sharp peaks, but a thin layer of plastic covered them.

She gripped Landon's upper arm and marched him to a quiet spot under a tree. Bemused, he let her pull him along.

A thin woman drowning in a yellow tunic laughed and called after them, "Ooh, someone's in trouble!"

"What in the Bright Above are you *doing*, Landon?" Ellis demanded. "Why are you wearing fake plastic ears over your real ears?"

Landon grinned again. "It makes the 'disguise' more believable."

Up close, Ellis could see smudges of purple makeup that matched his real skin tone on his face. She poked his cheek, and her fingertip came away indigo.

Landon rubbed the spot. "Ow. You need to clip your nails."

"This is insane!" Ellis exclaimed. "You'll expose the whole homestead!"

"Calm down! You're drawing attention."

Ellis, who was as red as Landon was purple, drew two deep breaths. One because she hated anyone telling her to calm down, and the second because he was right.

She growled. "*I'm* drawing attention? *Me?* That's what you have to say for yourself, *Blueberry Boy?*"

His lips twitched. "'Blueberry Boy?' Around here, I go by 'Seletherinol the Violet.'"

"What kind of name is *that?*"

"It's my elf name."

"Your 'elf name' is Landon Burton."

"Try telling King Henry that." He gestured at the man who had greeted Ellis, and King Henry raised a cheerful, meaty hand in response. "Apparently, 'Landon Burton' is a ridiculous name for an elf."

Ellis shook her head, but she knew what he meant. Elves in movies had names like Goltheniel, Sylvana, and Peppermint.

"Plus," Landon enthusiastically added, "I'm an *evil* elf, so having a good name is important."

Ellis frowned. "Why are you evil?"

"Because I have purple skin. They tell me that's how it works."

Ellis did not have time to unpack that. She surveyed the wooden picnic tables covered with weapons and the attendees' unusual outfits, and in the space of thirty seconds, she overheard three separate uses of the word "thou." A kid under a nearby tree swung a wooden longsword covered in foam. He looked like he was barely out of high school.

She pulled Landon's dagger from its sheath. The carved bone hilt gleamed in the sunlight, as did the moonsteel blade. It was a genuine drow weapon passed down by their grandfather. "What the hell is happening here?" she demanded. "Are you going to war?"

Landon nudged her. "Put that away, or we'll get in trouble. No naked blades. We're not going to war. We're *pretending* to. It's a game."

Her eyebrows drew together in confusion. "Where you pretend to kill each other?"

"Yeah, but with sparring and magic spells."

The blood drained from Ellis' face. "You're not showing them shadow magic, are you?" Not that Landon had much to show, although she tactfully did not point that out.

He shook his head and yanked a length of glitter-filled plastic tubing from his boot. "Not real magic, no, but I can take someone's eye out with this." He aimed it at a young woman who was staring shyly from behind a shield and cried, "*Oculus extractum!*"

The young woman shrieked and grabbed her left eye. Then she switched to her right eye. Then, she decided that it *had* hit her left eye. After a moment of faux agony, she grinned, waved, and returned to adjusting the buckle on her shield.

Ellis, who'd been wracking her brain for a mushroom ointment that would regrow an eye, relaxed and glared at Landon.

"I just learned that one!" he cheerfully told her, then added, "Like I said, no real magic. Just pretend."

"You enjoy pretending?"

"I enjoy not having to pretend." Landon stretched and admired his purple hands.

"You wouldn't have to pretend if you stayed home."

"When did you start quoting Dad?"

Ellis scowled, but King Henry shouted over the crowd before she could retort. "Good Seletherinol, bring thine indigo visage hither!"

Her scowl turned skeptical. "Is that even English?"

Landon shrugged, then waved at his liege lord. "One sec, Henry!" He quietly asked Ellis, "What did you want to talk to me about, anyway?"

Right. She'd had a reason for coming here that wasn't encountering a whole lot of crazy in one place. "I need to borrow your medallion. Pre-charged."

Landon raised an eyebrow. "So, when *I* need something, you say no for my own good, but when *you* need something, you expect me to drop everything and casually rob the Swallow's Nest?"

"You rob the Swallow's Nest all the time."

"For personal gain. Not to help you."

"What if I make it worth your while?"

"Will you help me find Errol?"

Ellis grumbled. "Are you *sure* that's what you want? You

MARTHA CARR & MICHAEL ANDERLE

wouldn't prefer, I dunno, gold? Jewels? A hot tub?" Any of those would be easier and more palatable.

Landon shook his head. "No thanks. Errol, or no deal."

Ellis considered the tradeoffs. She wasn't sure the medallion would work on Percy, and if it did, it wasn't guaranteed to work as expected. It might not do anything, or it might turn Percy purple.

Not to mention that Errol was bad news. Landon was thriving without him.

On the other hand, Percy was withering away in her apartment, and it was Ellis' fault he was a fugitive. Springing him from figurative house arrest would go a long way toward making up for that. Also, if Ellis didn't help Landon, he would undoubtedly track Errol down on his own.

She grimaced. "Fine. I'll help."

Landon's bright smile was contagious. "Awesome. If you stick around, I'll tell you everything you need to know at the victory march. We don't often get spectators. Unless you want to fight too? I have an extra pair of pointy ears in my bag. I'm Henry's royal warlock. I can get you a position at court, sis."

Now, there's a thought. A few years ago, she would have jumped at the chance to have pointed ears, even fake ones, but they looked uncomfortable, and they likely wouldn't match her skin tone. She assessed the opposing crowd, which was gathering around a bright yellow banner painted with a sun. She could take any of them in a fight. Hell, she could probably take *all* of them in a fight.

"If I join the battle, can I kick people in the face?" she asked hopefully.

Landon looked appalled. "Only if you cover your boots in Styrofoam."

"Where's the fun in that?"

King Henry shouted for Seletherinol again, and Landon anxiously looked at his blue banner. "You give me your word that you'll help me find Errol?"

Ellis did her best to look noble as she nodded. It worked well enough that Landon fished the gold medallion out of his pocket and pressed it into her hand. The metal vibrated with magical energy that crackled against her skin, just out of reach.

Landon put a second item in her hand: a small stoppered bottle carved from black stone and polished to a mirror finish. "I almost forgot. Trissa made this. She says it should help with your shadow magic. You're supposed to drink it."

"Now?"

Landon shook his head. "She said it's safe, but it might knock you out for a day or so. She said to sip it first and see how it goes."

"Tell her thanks." Ellis' fingers closed around the cool, heavy bottle, and Landon nodded and ran over to King Henry.

Warriors whooped, and the chatter grew agitated. Ellis retired to a picnic table on a nearby rise to spectate. Something tugged at her heart as she watched Landon grinning and waving his ridiculous glittering plastic tube and exchanging jokes with his friends.

It was one thing to see Landon and Errol prowling the LA streets at night, their drow faces half-concealed by hoods. It was a different experience to watch Landon in the sunlight, easily accepted by humans who looked nothing like him.

I'm jealous. It hit Ellis like an axe. A regular one, no Styrofoam needed. Even with his purple skin, her brother was thriving. What did that say about her? Maybe drow society hadn't excluded her because she looked different but because she wasn't likable.

Personal problems aside, Landon's easy, open warmth with his new friends was a good sign. Someday, Landon would be a drow elder, and if this kept up, he might not make the dark elves hide from human society.

Someone blew a horn, and the *real* battle began. The armies, which were as disorganized as real medieval armies, surged forward. Foam-tipped arrows flew in wobbly arcs, and people waved plastic wands and enthusiastically shouted faux magic words.

The two armies were evenly matched, but Henry's blue banner crawled forward foot by hard-fought foot as the yellow army fell to their attackers' well-padded blows. The "dead" soldiers lay where they fell, fidgeting and chatting softly, although a few jogged off the field to retrieve sweatshirts or bottles of water.

One small figure on the ground, a teenager named Wallace carrying twin foam daggers, got up after the battle moved past him. He raised his daggers and slunk toward Henry and Landon in a sneak attack. Ellis respected the ruse, but she couldn't let it stand when her brother was so close to winning.

"Landon!" Ellis shouted, then clapped a hand over her mouth. *Uh-oh. I'm invested.*

Wallace raised the daggers above his head and charged,

but Ellis' warning had reached Landon in time. Her brother's plastic tube-wand went up, and indistinguishable words echoed across the lawn.

Wallace half-heartedly shouted and grudgingly sank to the ground. When he was down for real, he glared at Ellis. "You're not even playing!"

"I'll have you know I was offered a position at court earlier."

Landon grinned. "That's right! She's in King Henry's retinue."

"In what capacity?" the kid demanded.

Ellis popped off her picnic table and sauntered over. "I'm the royal boot-wielder."

"That's not a job," Wallace protested.

"True. It's more a vocation." Ellis smiled brightly, and Landon laughed.

"Yer most welcome, lass," Henry shouted, "but I need my elf warlock!"

Landon raced back to Henry, and the kid on the ground glared at Ellis.

"You cheated," he complained.

"War is hell, kid."

He sat up and wrapped his arms around his knees. He looked so forlorn that she took pity on him. He couldn't have been older than fourteen.

"You should practice keeping your body behind your daggers," she told him. "Even if I hadn't warned Landon... er, Thingamajig the Purple—"

"Seletherinol the Violet," Wallace corrected.

"Yeah, him. Even if I hadn't warned him, you were wide open to attacks."

Instead of arguing with her or seeming insulted, he picked up his daggers and looked at them with interest, then swiped the air a few times.

She smiled. "Find me later. I'll give you some pointers."

Ellis meandered toward the fray and debated the best method for wrapping the toes of her boots in Styrofoam. By the time she reached the main cohort, the heat of battle had cooled, and it died a few minutes later. King Henry's army was victorious.

The warriors removed uncomfortable costume pieces while the court mages summoned beer from coolers they'd left in cars in the parking lot. Wallace poured an orange soda into a drinking horn, sipped it, and stared at Ellis.

"I think he has a crush on you," Landon whispered.

"He's just jealous of my dagger-fighting skills." Both were likely accurate.

King Henry had officially "lost an arm" in the battle. He cheerfully kept up the pretense by drinking from his pewter goblet with his right hand tied behind his back. Ellis accepted a delicate crystal goblet from the king.

"Have you got magic powers like your brother, lass?" the king asked.

Ellis paused.

"She's more of a hand-to-hand fighter," Landon offered.

Henry leaned in, interested. "Karate? Tae kwon do? Jiu-jitsu?"

Ellis shrugged. "I like kicking things."

The king laughed. "You're welcome back anytime."

She turned down a second drink, although Wallace eagerly offered to refill her goblet with orange soda.

Landon's steps were light as she walked him back to his bicycle. "Admit it. You had fun."

Ellis sighed and smiled. "Yeah, I had fun." She promised to come back, then narrowed her eyes. "If I'm tracking down Errol, I need to know everything. Where's the last place you saw him?"

"In the LA tunnels, but we texted for a while after that. He told me he'd moved to Topanga Canyon. The other sideshow performers live out there in a commune. I went once with my medallion, but they said he wasn't there. They gave me a weird vibe, too, like they were lying to me. Errol hasn't answered my texts in over a month."

"Okay. I'll check it out, but please understand I'm still not at full strength."

He nodded. "I'd appreciate anything you can find."

"I'll be in touch."

She bid him goodbye and headed for Granny, then frowned. Someone was sitting on her bike. Her anxiety only lessened a little when she recognized Charlie.

Had he come to apologize? He didn't need to sit on her bike to apologize. That wasn't cool. She greeted him by pushing him off Granny onto the lawn. Then she stood over him and planted her boot in his chest.

"I told you not to follow me."

Charlie held up his hands in surrender. "I know, I know. I'm sorry. I wanted to meet you on neutral ground."

Ellis removed her foot from his torso. When he stood, she instinctively moved to block his view of "Seletherinol the Violet." Charlie was already too obsessed with purple people.

She nervously fiddled with the medallion in her pocket. "You could have called. Or come to my apartment."

"I didn't think you would pick up, and like I said, I wanted neutral territory."

His pupils were wide, and he kept checking for escape routes. He was afraid she would hurt him. Ellis was offended but realized that his concern wasn't unfounded.

He hadn't brought his gun. Ellis wasn't sure what that meant.

Charlie nodded at a nearby station wagon. Wallace was watching them, open-mouthed. "In the future, I'd appreciate it if you didn't beat me up in front of kids."

"Wally, come on! You're late for your geometry tutor," a woman who was presumably his mother yelled from the front seat.

Ellis waved, and Wallace reluctantly pulled his legs into the car and closed the door. She rounded on Charlie. "What do you want?"

"It's an emergency. I wouldn't be here if it wasn't. Trust me." His tone suggested that he could conceive of many activities more pleasant than talking to Ellis Burton, like eating glass or pulling out his fingernails. Ellis waited. "Liza's missing."

"Your partner? I'm sorry, Charlie, but aren't you a detective? The kind with a shiny brass badge? Maybe you can use your many years of experience as an officer of the law to find her."

"I have. Liza's not at her apartment. She has a sister in town, Mariela, but she's not there, and Mariela hasn't heard anything. I think something's happened."

"Her closure and arrest rate are high, right?"

"Yeah."

"That means her 'making enemies' rate is equally high. It could be anyone."

"I'd agree with you, except that I talked to the captain about opening a case and pulling a few officers onto it. The new captain."

Ellis, who could still remember the sound of the gunshot that had killed Jericho, shivered. "I don't understand the connection."

"The captain said she took a leave of absence."

"Then what's the problem?"

"I think he's lying. I think something happened, or he did something to her."

"Why?"

"She wouldn't leave without telling me or her family. It's *way* out of character."

"Maybe she's pissed off at you."

"Liza's not the type to vanish without a word, even if she *is* mad at you. I'd know." His gaze was dark enough that Ellis suspected he knew from firsthand experience. "If she was that pissed off, she'd have said something. Yelled at me. Asked increasingly pointed questions. She wouldn't have just gone."

Ellis crossed her arms. "What do you want me to do about it?"

"I wanted to ask if you'd seen her. If you'd...done anything to her." He was afraid, but he stubbornly pressed on. "She thought I should have arrested you the first time we met. She was suspicious of our...interactions."

"'Interactions?' I would have called it a friendship, Charlie, but what do I know?"

Charlie looked down at his boots, chastened.

"I haven't seen her," Ellis told him gently. "But if I did hurt her, why would I tell you?"

"A lot of illogical things have happened to me this year." Charlie looked crumpled—bent under an invisible and heavy load.

An urge to ask him out for tacos or banana cream pie seized her, but she resisted it. If he thought she'd murdered his partner, dates were not in their future.

"If you see her, will you tell me?" Charlie asked.

"Of course, but I wouldn't get your hopes up."

He nodded and mumbled something like, "Thanks." As he left, he glanced at the new license plate on her bike. Ellis wondered if she should swap it out, but she didn't think she needed to. If Charlie came for her, he wouldn't outsource the job.

She patted Granny's fuel tank as she straddled the bike. The gold medallion was heavy in her pocket, but it was the middle of the afternoon. Time to hunt for the errant Errol. "What do you say to a nice, long ride, old girl?"

CHAPTER FIFTEEN

She started with the sideshow performers' commune. The ride to the canyon was less pleasant than it had been the other day. She took the curves fast to save time, not for the thrill.

Landon's directions led her up a brush-covered hill on a series of switchbacks to a small turnoff between two luxury mansions. The path was an overgrown tunnel of vegetation that spat her out into a shallow valley that ended in an open field bordered by woods. A stream gurgled to her right, and on her left sat a series of unusual round cabins.

When Ellis parked her bike and removed her helmet, a pale-skinned, pink-eyed woman emerged from the nearest dwelling. Ellis recognized her from the photo Landon had shown her, although the photo hadn't captured her striking beauty or her remarkable curves, which swayed under a silky white dress. The only contrast was the black choker at her throat. Snakes were not the only thing she charmed.

MARTHA CARR & MICHAEL ANDERLE

The choker moved as the woman approached, and Ellis' breath caught. It wasn't a necklace but a sinuous slender snake.

"This is Onyx," the woman explained by way of greeting. Her fingers brushed the snake. The overall effect was unsettling, and Ellis backed up. "Not a fan? That's unfortunate. I'm Ophidia. Snakes are my line of work."

Through the open door of the round cabin behind Ophidia, Ellis spied glass tanks glittering under heat lamps.

"You should meet Percy," Ellis replied.

"Who's Percy?"

"The animal kingdom's biggest fan." The whip-like snake slithered, and Ellis' stomach twisted into a knot.

Ophidia lowered a pair of white sunglasses onto her nose. "I see. Can I help you?"

"I'm looking for Errol," Ellis replied, "although you might not know him by that name."

Ophidia frowned. "What does he look like?"

No one in history had asked an easier question. "He's purple."

Recognition lit the woman's face, and she glanced at a tent in the background. "You're talking about Shadow. What did you call him?"

Ellis ignored her and stepped closer to Ophidia. "Where is he?" She was a foot taller than the other woman, but the snake charmer wasn't rattled. Jumpiness would be a serious disadvantage in her vocation.

Ophidia crossed her pale arms and sized Ellis up. Finally, she pressed her lips together and nodded. "Come with me."

The woman moved with the same slow undulation as

the snake around her neck, sliding across the ground in smooth curves. Ellis would bet significant amounts of money that her act was very popular.

"When Shadow showed up, I worried that Dragonman would complain. There are rivalries even among sideshow performers. They'd either kill each other or become best friends. Fortunately, I guessed right."

"I take it they didn't kill each other?"

"No. As it turns out, Los Angeles is big enough for two tattooed men. Although Shadow still hasn't told us where he got his work done or who does his hair."

"Probably somewhere super underground," Ellis responded dryly.

Ophidia gazed at Ellis, inviting further explanation. When Ellis said nothing, she shrugged. "You're no doubt right."

She led Ellis to one of the round structures. It had wooden walls and a thatched roof and was unlike any other human building Ellis had seen. "Yurts are practical," Ophidia commented. "They're modeled after Mongolian tents. The wooden ones aren't as portable, but they have a certain flair."

An etched bell hung on a cord near the door and occasionally rang in the light breeze. Ophidia pulled the cord in a complex series of long and short tones, waited a moment, and pushed open the door.

The interior was one big room. All the furniture was pushed against the wood-paneled walls, and a sweet-smelling haze drifted from a decorative censer on a bookshelf. Woven shades covered the windows.

Two figures stood at the far curve of the room, indistinct in the haze until Ellis blinked and squinted. On the left was the infamous Dragonman. He wasn't large, but the scale tattoos marching across his body made him imposing.

The other man glittered in the low light. His piercings were arresting. Ellis had seen a wide variety of body jewelry in Los Angeles, but none was like his. Rings and studs protruded from every inch of skin. Long lines of rings marched down the sides of his neck onto his shoulders. More piercings tented the thin fabric of his tank top.

There was so much going on visually that Ellis didn't initially notice the stiletto in his hand. Ellis stepped back, but in one smooth movement, Ophidia grasped her shoulder and pressed the tip of another knife into Ellis' spine.

Ellis' muscles tensed as she prepared to dive away from the blade.

"I wouldn't do that if I were you," Ophidia warned. "This blade is coated in banded krait venom. It's hard to recover from a stab wound with a paralyzed diaphragm."

"Search her, Cush." Dragonman's tongue flicked between his lips. It was forked.

Ophidia's breath blew hot in Ellis' ear while the metal-covered man patted her down and fished through her pockets. "This is the Human Pincushion. Everyone calls him 'Cush.'"

Ellis grimaced when Cush relieved her of her boot knife, but she couldn't stop staring at Dragonman. She was enchanted by his complete transformation. She wondered how long it had taken and how painful it had been.

I could be purple.

Ellis set the thought aside. She'd consider extreme body modification when she wasn't being held at poisoned knifepoint.

Cush casually inspected Ellis' belongings. He determined that her cell phone was locked. He looked at her key ring, then searched her wallet. When he picked up the small black stone bottle, Ellis made a strangled noise. The bottle was her best chance of regaining her shadow magic.

He unstopped the bottle and waved it under his nose. "What is this?"

"I wouldn't advise sniffing strange bottles." Ophidia's voice dripped disapproval. Working with venom made a woman paranoid.

Cush jerked his head back. "*Is* it poison?"

"No." Ellis left it at that.

Dragonman meandered over and plucked the bottle from his friend's hands. He rotated it, watched the liquid shift behind the glass, then pocketed it.

"You can't take that!" Ellis protested. She surged forward, but Ophidia pulled her back.

"To the victor go the spoils." Ophidia finished the word with a long hiss. Ellis wondered whether it was an affectation or a byproduct of working with snakes.

Cush rifled through her wallet. "No ID," he grunted. He left her cash where it was, which was something. He examined the gold key to the Bromeliad's sub-basement but, finding nothing to unlock among Ellis' belongings, deposited it in a handwoven basket on a round copper table with everything else.

"How mysterious." Ophidia delightedly murmured.

"Does she have a badge?" Dragonman crossed his arms.

His pale purple T-shirt contrasted with his imposing tattoos.

Ellis frowned. "A badge?"

"FBI? CIA? NSA? Interpol?"

Ophidia rolled her eyes. "She's not Interpol."

"You don't know that," Ellis cut in. "I *could* be Interpol." *We'll ignore the fact that I don't know what Interpol is.*

She sternly glared at Dragonman and Cush. Dragonman was wiry and scrappy, but she could take him. Cush's visually impressive jewelry would put him at a serious disadvantage in a fight. All she had to do was grab a handful and pull.

That left Ophidia and her purportedly poisoned knife. The snake handler was clearly the group's leader.

"Didn't see any badges. She doesn't have any more weapons, either," Cush reported.

"You won't say that when my boot hits your face," Ellis retorted. The knifepoint pressed into her back and deflated her smirk. "Watch it."

"You don't give the orders here," Ophidia tartly replied.

Ellis tried to look meek, which did not come naturally.

"What do you want with Shadow?" Ophidia asked.

She had no reason to hide the truth. "He's friends with my brother. Landon's worried about him, so he asked me to swing by."

Cush and Dragonman exchanged worried glances, but the pressure on the knife relaxed. Ellis considered taking advantage of that, but these people struck her as more worried and protective than dangerous.

"Go get him," Ophidia ordered after a long pause.

Cush nodded and hurried out, rattling as he went.

Ophidia steered Ellis to a woven chair and pushed her into it, then circled back and loomed over Ellis. Her grip on her knife was practiced, and a viscous, oily liquid glistened on the blade. The banded krait venom threat hadn't been a bluff.

Errol was a chaos magnet. Bad luck had followed him from the drow homestead to the LA tunnels and Topanga Canyon. Why were his new friends protecting him?

"Any shows coming up?" Ellis ventured. If she could build rapport, they might divulge information. Dragonman ignored her, and Ophidia rolled her eyes.

Ellis resigned herself to waiting. It wasn't long before purple flashed at the bottom of the blinds, and the door opened. No one bothered to ring the bell this time.

Errol stepped in and Cush followed on his heels. When Ellis greeted him by name, his eyebrows drew together, and he winced.

"'Errol,' is it?" Ophidia was amused. "How old-fashioned."

"My name's *Shadow*," Errol replied, irritated.

"It's okay, man. We didn't think Shadow was your birth name." Dragonman offered a comforting smile.

Ellis noticed as the bully stepped forward that his ears were smooth ovals. Pale scar tissue betrayed the surgery.

Errol's gaze slid over Ophidia's white skin and lingered on the snake around her neck in obvious infatuation. He tore his attention away, crossed his arms, and glared at Ellis. "What are you doing here, Tomato Face?"

"She said her name was Ellis," Cush protested. Not the sharpest piercing in the shop.

"Tomato Face is my birth name. I go by Ellis now." Ellis tried not to smirk when Ophidia stifled laughter.

"What are you doing here?" Errol repeated.

"Keeping a promise," Ellis replied. "Would you mind calling off your friends? I'd rather not be shanked today."

Errol sighed. He looked like he'd rather lose the rest of his ears than send Ophidia outside, but he reluctantly nodded. "Ellis is okay, guys. You can leave us alone."

Ophidia smiled, and Errol swallowed hard. When she touched his arm with the tips of her colorless fingers, Ellis thought he would spontaneously combust. She recognized that look since she'd seen it on Charlie's face. She pushed the thought away.

"Are you sure, Shadow?" Ophidia asked.

"Yeah."

"Suit yourself. Cush will stay outside. Shout if you have any trouble."

Errol nodded, then blurted, "She's just a friend!"

Ophidia's silky smile widened. She patted Errol's shoulder twice, then moved toward the door. "Dinner's at seven," she called over her shoulder on her way out.

"I'm making beets!" Cush added.

Only after Ophidia disappeared did Errol seem capable of conversation. His expression landed somewhere between worried and annoyed.

"Your friends seem nice," Ellis drawled.

"They *are* nice," Errol said protectively. "You of all people shouldn't judge them because they look different."

He was twitchy. Ellis guessed he hadn't expected his past to catch up with him.

"In my defense, I'm mostly judging them for taking my

stuff and holding me at poisoned knifepoint." She sprang from her chair. Errol shied away, and she crossed to the woven basket and retrieved her belongings. "Dragonman took something from me."

"He probably thought it was dangerous."

It was. "Why have you been blowing off Landon's calls?"

He rubbed the smooth edge of his ear meditatively until he noticed Ellis watching and stopped. "I'm making a new life for myself. I wanted a fresh start."

Errol appeared to consider Ellis in a new light. "You know, maybe it's good you're here. I'll tell you what. I'll text Landon now and tell him I'm okay."

He retrieved a cell phone from his pocket and tapped it. Errol scowled when he noticed Ellis grinning. "What?"

"It took me forever to learn how to use my phone, too, that's all."

"Everyone here thinks it's impressive that I'm so 'off-the-grid.' They think it's *counterculture*." Errol cursed as he poked the uncooperative screen. "There. I texted Landon. Why don't we go for a walk? There's a rise at the top of the property with a terrific view of the ocean. Stick around for dinner, and I'll talk to Dragonman about your thing."

Ellis shrugged. "That won't make Ophidia jealous?"

"It might if I'm lucky." He ran a hand through his silver hair, then hurried out the door.

Ellis fired off a quick text to Landon, too.

You're welcome.

A walk sounded nice, and despite their rocky start,

Errol's new friends were interesting. Maybe a stroll would relax him enough to spill a few beans.

Ellis' phone buzzed as she headed for the door. It was Landon.

???

Ellis paused and frowned.

Did you get Errol's text?

The three dots flashed briefly, then his reply came through.

No. Did you find him?

Ellis exited the yurt and found Errol pacing a few feet away. Why would he lie to her? *You don't know that he's lying.* His message could have been delayed. Service was probably sketchy this far out in the country.

When Ellis drew up beside him, his phone beeped. Errol's forehead wrinkled when he glanced at the screen. Then he forced a smile.

"Who was that?" she asked innocently.

"Landon. He said he's happy to hear from me." Three more texts flickered on the screen in quick succession. He scanned them, then shoved his phone into his pocket. "Let's go."

Errol grabbed her arm hard enough to dig his fingers in, and Ellis yelped. "Ow!"

His grip loosened. "Sorry. We have to move fast, or we'll miss the sunset."

Without waiting for her to follow, he marched around the yurt toward a gap in the foliage. It would be dark soon.

Ellis wished she had a weapon. She thought she could beat Errol in hand-to-hand combat, but if he was armed, she'd be outmatched without access to her shadow magic. Errol had never been strong in that arena, but right now, even he was stronger than her, although he didn't know that.

Granny glinted from the other side of the clearing. If she caught Errol off-guard with a disabling kick, she could sprint to the Harley before he caught up, but then she wouldn't learn why he was lying or who he was texting.

Charlie Morrissey floated through her head. *The thing about questions is that sometimes they have answers.*

She followed Errol into the brush. She never could resist a secret.

CHAPTER SIXTEEN

The temperature dropped as the sun dipped behind the hills, and the yellowing foliage of the scrub brush and oak trees was thin. Ellis was glad she was wearing her motorcycle jacket. The narrow trail followed a series of rough stone steps up a hill beside a creek.

Near the top, Errol glanced back. His gaze was cold and hard, so Ellis knew she was in trouble, but she smiled innocently in return. She expected a fight, but Errol kept climbing.

She silently pulled out her phone, dialed Landon's number, and slipped it back into her pocket. She prayed he would pick up and keep his mouth shut.

"What did Landon say?" Ellis called after Errol. Errol stopped dead and turned around, and Ellis knelt and pretended to tie her left boot. "The texts you got at the yurt. Is he pissed?"

"He said he was glad you found me."

"That's all? He was *really* worried about you."

Errol ignored her. "Let's go."

Ellis continued "re-tying" her boot but looked up. "No."

"What?"

She watched his hands, ready to move if he grabbed a weapon. "Why are you lying?"

"I'm not," Errol protested, but he looked so squirrelly that Ellis laughed.

He didn't appreciate the joke. He stalked over, grabbed her arm, and pulled. His fingers dug in hard enough to draw blood, and Ellis gasped. She had become accustomed to fighting humans, and Errol's drow strength shocked her. He'd been an asshole, but he'd never hurt her.

If she had anything to say about it, he wasn't about to start. She allowed Errol to yank her to her feet and used the momentum to drive a knee toward his groin, but he realized her plan and twisted away, then gripped her arm even harder.

"Errol, *stop!*" Ellis hoped to the Mother Beneath that Landon had picked up the call, but with the phone in her pocket, she couldn't tell. "Where are we going?"

"I told you, there's a clearing at the top of the hill."

He tugged, and Ellis stumbled forward two steps. "*Fuck* your sunset. I'm not going anywhere with you."

"Like hell, you're not!"

"Let me go, or I'll take your hand off with shadow magic."

"You never would have let Ophidia hold you at knife-point if you could do that," Errol snarled. He yanked Ellis up three of the shallow stone steps. Something buzzed in the distance.

"Why are you doing this? Landon will never forgive you if you hurt me!"

Errol kept pulling. Ellis was concerned he would pull her arm from its socket. She whimpered when his grip forced her tendons into odd angles, and she decided to try a new tactic. "I don't have any money. You won't get anything from me."

He turned wide, sunken eyes on her. They weren't angry. They were sad.

"What are you doing, Shadow?" Ophidia slithered out of the brush behind them with a soft crackling of leaves.

Errol dropped Ellis' arm like it was on fire and implored Ophidia with his gaze for a forgiveness that was not forthcoming.

Ophidia's knife was back in her hand, but Ellis was not its target. "Explain yourself."

"I can't!" Errol desperately replied.

Ellis considered the empty trail behind Ophidia. Could she hold her own against Errol? She didn't think Errol would hurt the woman since he was head-over-heels for her.

Ellis ran. Her thick-soled boots kicked up dirt and pebbles, and she fumbled for Granny's key in her pocket. She'd kept her promise to Landon. He couldn't be angry with her for refusing to be murdered in the woods.

Ellis had almost reached the clearing when a gunshot stopped her in her tracks. As soon as she stopped moving, the whir of helicopter blades assaulted her ears and nearly covered a scream from someone in the commune.

The helicopter was so close that she could feel the vibrations under her feet. She looked up through the trees and spotted the black craft skimming the treetops as it flew up the hillside. Was it heading for the clearing Errol had mentioned?

Another gunshot and another scream. Shit was going down in the compound. Errol was an asshole, but his new friends didn't deserve to lose their lives because they hadn't figured that out.

Ellis sprinted into the open field in the direction of the second scream. Whoever was hurt was in the cabins along the creek.

A clod of dirt exploded at her feet. Someone was shooting at her. Ellis cursed, picked up her pace, and zigzagged to make herself a challenging target. She hoped the gunner didn't get lucky.

The back of the cabin had a small glass window, and Ellis reached for a nearby pool of shadows collecting under the vegetation. The dark power brushed her palms and slipped through. *It was worth a shot.*

She couldn't afford to slow down, so she folded her leather-clad arms across her face and dove through the window.

The glass splintered around her, and she landed with a *thud* and rolled over the wooden flooring. Someone shouted in fear rather than pain.

Ellis shook shards of glass out of her blue-black hair and opened her eyes. The room was bright and surprisingly warm, and after adjusting to the surprise, Ellis understood why.

She was in Ophidia's building. Reptile tanks covered the walls from floor to ceiling, and heat lamps blazed inside them. Behind a thick glass panel inches from her face, a snake as thick as her wrist coiled. It shook a rattle on the end of its tail and bared its fangs.

Ellis backed away but stopped as a shadow loomed over her. It was Cush, and he looked pissed. The bright lights of the reptile house gleamed not only off his piercings but also off the blade of the axe he clutched tightly.

"Who the hell are you, and why are you shooting at us?"

Oh, for fuck's sake. "I'm Ellis Burton. Errol…uh, *Shadow* and I grew up together. He was a bully to me during my childhood, to be honest. And I'm not shooting at you!"

Cush scowled. "Why should I trust you?"

A red dot appeared on his chest, and Ellis kicked Cush's feet out from under him. He swung the axe, but his movements were awkward, and Ellis caught the wooden shaft as the rifle fired.

A reptile tank exploded in a rain of glass. Cush yelled and tried to wrench the axe away from Ellis, but she held on and hissed, "I'm not the enemy."

A third shot shattered another tank, and its resident slithered out and along a shelf. Ellis spotted the label on a shard, and her eyes widened.

Eastern coral snake. Venomous. Do not handle.

Her heart pounded, but she forced herself to remain calm and think about what Percy would do. She closed her eyes and pictured his face. The mental image came complete with a ludicrous tracksuit.

Snakes do not want to hurt you. Hurting a predator took energy, and snakes preferred to spend their energy finding a nice hot rock to sleep on.

Cush interrupted her train of thought with a hollow, "Oh, shit. That's the krait." She followed his gaze to a yellow- and black-banded snake twisting across an aluminum shelf.

They backed across the glass-covered floor. Movement through an unbroken window caught Ellis' eye, and she spied a black-clad figure advancing toward the cabin with a high-tech rifle trained on the window.

She ducked and yanked Cush down with her. "We have to leave."

He shook his head vigorously, which sounded like the rattlesnake's tail rattling. Tears welled in the big man's eyes. "Dragonman went out that door, and they shot him. I think he's dead."

Ellis chanced popping up to peek through the window. Bile rose in her throat when she saw a dark, unmoving shape on the ground. Farther off, two black vans were parked near Granny, and a soldier in black fatigues raised binoculars toward Ellis' window.

She dropped back down and cautiously crossed the room to another window that opened on the woods. She listened closely and heard something moving in the vegetation. She caught a flash of black fabric in the trees.

"We're surrounded," Ellis whispered.

"Who the fuck are those people?" Cush hissed back. "Why did they kill Dragonman?"

"I don't know, but I think Shadow called them here."

Cush's eyes widened.

Welcome to Betrayal, buddy. Population: us.

Ellis' gaze landed on the snake in the room's biggest enclosure. It was hard to estimate its size, given that it was half-hidden in a fake log, but she'd bet it was at least eight feet long. It had pale bands on its dark scales, and where its neck met its head, its skin flared in a hood.

The note on this enclosure read *King cobra. Venomous. Do not handle.*

An additional Post-it note with cursive writing had been stuck on top.

I'm serious about this one, guys. Don't do it.

Ellis sprawled across the wooden floor on her back. The pinpricks of the heat lamps burned her retinas. *Snakes don't want to hurt you. Not without a good reason.*

"I guess I'd better give them a reason," she whispered.

"What?" Cush was curled into a ball in the corner with his arms around his knees.

"I have an idea. It's crazy, but it's our best shot."

He whimpered.

"These people are professionals. Even if we make it to the tree line without being shot, they'll hunt us down. I have *one* idea. It's far-fetched, but I think it'll work. Don't freak out."

Before she could second-guess herself, she unhooked the lid of the king cobra's glass terrarium and popped it open. Then she reached above her head, clapped three times, and said, "I need your help."

"What the hell are you *doing?*" Cush demanded.

Ellis shushed him and repeated, "I need your help."

"Help with *what?*" Cush was shivering with fear. It made his piercings rattle.

"Not you. I'm talking to the snakes," she hissed.

Ellis' stomach felt like it wanted to leap up her throat when the thick rope of the cobra's body slithered up the side of its cage and out into the room. It moved with steady intention, keeping the front three feet of its body aloft and its fangs bared.

A thousand calm lectures from Percy couldn't dissolve the hard knot of fear in her guts. It was a primeval terror. *Get over it, Ellis.*

Ellis raised her hands and clapped three times again. "Do you know what that means?" This time, Cush said nothing, although he caught his breath, and his piercings rattled louder.

The snake slithered closer. If it struck, it would hit her knee.

"Does Ophidia keep stores of antivenin?" Ellis whispered.

"She says it's a crutch that keeps handlers from being careful."

Of course. Ellis sucked in a breath. They'd be out of luck if the snakes bit them. On the other hand, that would also be true for their attackers.

Ellis focused on the cobra. "People are coming for us. They are not friends. They want to hurt you. They want to hurt Ophidia."

She had no idea if the snakes returned their handler's affection. They didn't think like humans, but it was worth a shot.

"Please attack the people wearing black," she requested. The cobra coiled, then hissed. Ellis couldn't be sure, but she thought it nodded.

"Help me open the enclosures," Ellis told Cush.

"Are you *insane?*"

"Probably. I also want to live."

Ellis ignored the labels on the terrariums as she popped

their lids open. More than half had warning symbols, so she opened those first.

Another gunshot blasted a hole in the wall as they finished their campaign for reptilian freedom. Ellis grabbed Cush and pulled him to the floor with her. "Time to play dead."

The wind whistled through the bullet hole and rustled Ellis' hair. She'd managed to lay her face on a shard of glass, and the cut stung.

Heavy-booted footsteps approached. Scales tickled her hand, then slithered over her ankle. The snake was warm and dry, and the small movements of its vertebrae felt eerie. Ellis did her best not to shudder.

She desperately wished she had the potion Trissa had made for her. She might be able to retrieve it if it was still in Dragonman's pocket.

Another snake touched Ellis' hand, and her eyes opened. Before she shut them again, she saw a diamond-back rattlesnake undulating toward the door.

"Don't let me down, my slithery friends," she murmured.

The footsteps crunched across the ground, then paused. The commandos kicked the door in with a crash, and splinters joined the glass shards in Ellis' hair. In the brief silence that followed, there was a sharp rattle, then a hiss of pain.

"What the *fuck?*" the intruder groaned.

The whispered response was so soft that even Ellis' drow hearing barely caught it. An earpiece, she guessed.

"A fucking snake just bit me," the man explained. Glass crunched under his foot, and a snake slithered over Ellis' outstretched arm faster than she thought was possible. "Stop!" A throaty hiss preceded a scream.

The voice on the comm whispered.

"No. I'm okay, I just…" The floorboards creaked, then shook with a heavy impact.

Ellis risked opening her eyes. The soldier was on his knees, staring in disbelief at the snake dangling from his leg by its fangs. Two white-ringed dots adorned its outstretched hood, connected by a black-outlined arc. From behind, the hooded cobra looked like it was smiling.

"There's two of them." The man huffed. "Wait, four." His eyes were wet and unfocused. "No…no MECs."

The men who had attacked Morrissey's captain had called her an MEC. She'd been invisible at the time.

Ellis strained to hear the response over the earpiece. "Kill them," the person ordered.

"C-copy that." The soldier looked at his gun for a long time as though he was trying to remember what he was supposed to do with it.

Ellis decided to act before he remembered. She hoped there were no easily startled pit vipers on her as she stood in a single movement.

The soldier wordlessly stammered. A ski mask covered his face, but the skin around his eyes was dark and puffy. He sluggishly raised his automatic rifle, and Ellis kicked it away. He flailed, and the cobra on his leg detached, hissed, and slithered into a corner.

"Thank you. That's enough," Ellis told the cobra. With luck, it hadn't developed a taste for human flesh.

She yanked the earpiece off the soldier. It crackled, then went dead.

Ellis toppled the man and pinned him with a knee to his chest. "Who are you?"

Tears leaked from his eyes, and his mouth opened and closed uselessly.

Ellis shook his collar. "What's an MEC?"

He didn't answer. She grabbed his hands and found what she expected: a heavy gold ring bearing a half-moon surrounded by two concentric circles.

The soldier moaned and fell silent. His open eyes were glassy.

Ellis retrieved his rifle. She looked from him to Cush, who was still on the floor. Then she checked around him for snakes. One dangled off the shelf, but she saw none near the large sideshow performer.

"Cush?" she whispered. "Sit up. Slowly."

Cush's fearful gaze landed on the mottled, bloated soldier. "Is he dead?"

"If he isn't now, he will be soon. Take off your clothes."

"*What?*"

"Swap clothing with this guy."

"Why?"

"I need you to fetch something for me." She didn't see any way of getting her and Cush out of a situation with armed commandos and helicopters unless Trissa's potion restored her shadow magic.

"Remember that bottle Dragonman took from me? It's in his pocket. I need it. If they think you're with them, they won't shoot you."

She peered at the dead soldier. The material of his bodysuit shone. *More lightsilk. Shit.* She stepped back, then froze at a rattle from behind her. Caught between a snake and a lightsilk bodysuit.

"Undress him," she told Cush.

"What? Why can't you help?"

She borrowed a page from Ophidia's book and put authority in her voice. "Just do it!" She shook the rifle for emphasis, although she aimed it at the floor.

It was enough. Cush was not a natural leader. He relieved the dead operative of his fatigues, boots, bullet-proof vest, and ski mask. Two piercings snagged on the complicated body armor, but that only slightly delayed the process.

Ellis handed him the rifle. "Don't point it at anyone you don't want dead. When you leave this building, point at your earpiece and wave. Don't rush. Go to Dragonman's body, grab the bottle, and bring it back here. Do you understand?"

"I don't understand *anything!*" he complained.

"Ear. Bottle. Cabin. Slow and steady."

Cush nodded uncertainly, then, ungainly in his new gear, stumbled out. *Well, he supposedly got bitten by a snake. I guess that's fair.*

Ellis followed Cush's footsteps with her ears. He didn't rattle, muffled as he was in the gear. When they stopped, she knew he was at the body. This was the dangerous part. If they suspected foul play, they'd shoot.

Silence. A minute later, she heard running. *Stupid.* Running made people look suspicious.

Cush burst through the door with the bottle gripped in one hand. "I have—" A gunshot rang out, and Cush fell forward.

Ellis cursed and pulled him in by his sleeve, which burned her hand. She dragged him across the floor, then slammed the door.

There was a crater in the middle of his back. It didn't look like it was bleeding.

"Did I get shot?" Cush didn't sound mortally wounded, but adrenaline did crazy things.

"Yes, but I think the armor stopped the bullet. Take off your vest."

Ellis stepped away as he removed the upper half of the bodysuit and bared his back to her. To the right of his spine, a bullet was wedged in his T-shirt above a metal ring. The piercing was lightly bleeding, but the titanium ring had protected him from the last of the bullet's force.

Ellis pulled the slug out and handed it to Cush. "A souvenir to remind you of the first time metal *didn't* go through your body."

Cush took it. "Ellis. Dragonman."

She gripped his arm. "I'm so sorry."

He shook his head. "No. He's *alive*. He's wounded, but he's alive."

Ellis bit her lip. Gunshot victims didn't last long without help. She had to act.

She gently uncurled Cush's fingers from the black stone bottle, unstopped it, and chugged the contents.

CHAPTER SEVENTEEN

The liquid was thick and colder than it should have been after sitting in Dragonman's pocket. It cooled Ellis' throat and coated her mouth with an earthy, mineral taste.

Would it work? It might be a bust. Worse, it could poison her. Drinking poison in a room full of venomous snakes had a certain irony.

Ellis' fingers and toes went cold, and shadows obscured her vision. She felt as though she'd plunged into water deeper than sunlight could reach.

Shadow magic surrounded her. It swirled in every corner, filtered through the dark windows, and poured between the cracks in the cabin's walls. Everything that wasn't light was hers, and she drew it into herself.

Terror filled Cush's face. Ellis held up a hand to console him and gasped.

She was purple, or rather, her skin pulsed with purple swirls. Vibrant lilac and mauve whirled in patterns that broke apart and re-formed like dancing bruises.

Ellis wrapped herself and Cush in a thick blanket of

invisibility. Now, they had to escape the cabin. If they opened the front door or the windows, the attackers would shoot first and ask questions later. She needed a big distraction.

She cackled and gathered torrents of shadow magic in her fists. She had just the thing.

"Stay close, but don't touch me," Ellis told Cush. He nodded, unable to tear his gaze off the swirls on her skin. She suspected she wouldn't have to tell him twice. She noted that his legs crackled with energy where they were covered by lightsilk.

She stretched her arms out and dissolved the walls and roof of the cabin. Normally, an undertaking like that would exhaust her, but it was like over-inflating a balloon. The resistance lessened until *pop!* The wood was gone.

The heat lamps fizzled into darkness and the electricity failed as Ellis' stunt took out the wiring along with the walls. The night air breezed through the freestanding racks of glass tanks.

Ellis trotted toward the tree line. It would be harder to maintain invisibility in thick vegetation, but the cover would help if their assailants blanketed the forest with bullets.

She heard no movement behind her. She turned back to see that Cush was stationary.

"We have to go back for Dragonman."

Ellis looked at Dragonman's body, which was a dark lump in the twilight. "Are you sure he's still alive?"

"We have to check," Cush insisted.

Ellis groaned and turned around.

The magic buoyed her steps as though it was pulling

her off the ground. The purple on her hands was deepening, and the shadows were becoming denser and spreading into her fingers. She was filling with shadow magic.

Two black-clad figures crept across the field toward the concrete slab that had been under the cabin, guns in hand. Ellis made a wide arc away from the men's position. She wanted to sprint away, but Cush couldn't move as fast as she could, so they crept across the clearing until Ellis could stretch the shadow magic to Dragonman.

The exertion was minimal. She felt drunk with power. A shout from the black van barely broke through the heady, invincible feeling.

"What the fuck? The tattooed guy disappeared!" a woman exclaimed.

She sounded familiar, but Ellis didn't have time to match it to a face since the two soldiers had changed course.

Ellis hoped the shadow magic would muffle her voice as she yelled, "Get down!"

She dropped as the attackers opened fire. Bullets whistled over her head as she army-crawled toward Dragonman. When she reached him, she checked the pulse on his neck. It was faint but there.

The two soldiers were fifty feet from Ellis and Dragonman. One, a woman, judging by her size and gait, raised her rifle for another volley, but her companion put a hand up to stop her. He pulled a weapon off his belt that Ellis had hoped never to see again.

The lightsilk confetti gun.

The shadows swirling in Ellis' vision turned into a crimson haze of anger that spread like a pool of blood. The shadows pressed against her skull, and she howled with rage.

She shot out her right hand and blasted shadow magic from her palm in a thick rope, more than she'd ever accessed at once. More than she thought it was possible to access.

The magic blasted the funnel-shaped gun into a metallic mist. The soldier screamed and the woman stared in horror as blood sprayed from his severed wrist. She leveled her rifle at the "empty" clearing.

Ellis whipped the magic toward the automatic weapon. She was gaining precision as she learned to wield the torrent of power and was able to slice the rifle out of the woman's hands and chop the gun barrel in half.

Her enemy was disarmed. *Not to mention unhanded.* Ellis involuntarily giggled, the noise pushed out of her by the shadow magic that heaved like ocean waves.

Ellis ripped two wide strips off Dragonman's T-shirt and knotted them into a makeshift bandage. She pressed another piece of fabric against the wound, then wrapped the bandage around his torso. She had to blink rapidly to keep her vision clear of the shadows that pressed in on all sides.

She tied the bandage off, threw Dragonman over her shoulder, and made for the woods on a flood of magic. Cush followed.

Ellis' feet were cold. The shadow magic was flushing the warmth from her body like an icy river, and it was growing more powerful by the second. Dragonman weighed nothing. He was air on her shoulder, held aloft by magic as much as her muscles.

The tsunami of magic intensified when Ellis reached the trees, amplified by the darkness among the vegetation. She struggled to keep her balance as power buffeted her.

She was in trouble. This was too much magic for one person to control. It would dissolve her from the inside out if she didn't relieve the pressure soon.

Ellis flung a dense ball of shadow magic into the forest, and an oak tree disappeared in a shower of sawdust. The pain in her skull lessened, and she could see and hear again.

The helicopter's blades chattered above her as it came over to investigate the exploded tree.

A small, insistent voice pushed through the shadows. A man was saying her name. Ellis rubbed her face hard to clear her vision, but her face was ice-cold and her hands were colder. When her left hand touched Dragonman, he shivered.

The pressure of the shadow magic was increasing faster. Ellis blasted two more trees, but it barely made a dent.

Her ears picked up faint shouts from overhead, and she glanced up to see the barrel of a large gun pointing out of the helicopter at the nearest exploded tree. Its discharge was a *pop* of compressed air rather than the combustive *bang* of gun or a grenade exploding.

The air sparkled with tiny silver ball bearings, and each globe had a fluttering tail of fabric. Ellis recognized the sheen in the moonlight as lightsilk.

How dare they? Fury welled inside her, and she lifted her hands above her head. A vast cloud of shadow magic rushed to meet the glittering hail, dissolved tree branches, and blocked the starlight. When it met the lightsilk-bearing spheres, it dissolved the metal but it did nothing to the silk strands, which continued their slow yet inexorable descent.

Ellis ran. The shadow magic surge was accelerating exponentially. Her vision went black as she leaped over a fallen log, and when her foot landed awkwardly, she tumbled. Dragonman moaned when she dropped him, and he rolled across the forest floor.

If the shadow magic didn't dissipate, Ellis would die. The magic would eat her from the inside until she was a hollow bag of skin, and she would take Topanga Canyon with her.

Ellis screamed, "Cush! *Cush!* Where are you?"

A warm hand grabbed her flailing arm. He was closer than she expected. "I'm here! What do we do?"

Cush had removed his lightsilk shirt, but he was still wearing the pants. Ellis fumbled for his ankle and grabbed the hem.

It was like touching a brand. Heat flensed the shadow magic from Ellis' body, and she screamed as white fire replaced the cold darkness. She was a human torch, and everything around her was dripping, molten pain like lava, but she held onto Cush's ankle until he seemed to melt under her fingertips.

She released her grip. It felt like her fingers would disintegrate into ash as the darkness rushed back. Not the swirling shadow magic, but a sweet blanket of oblivion.

Ellis passed out.

When she opened her eyes, the pain had subsided

enough for her to see, although it wasn't gone. A purple face swam in her vision.

"*Errol?*" She thrashed and slapped the ground, hunting for a rock or a stick she could jam into his stupid, evil, disloyal face.

"No, sis. It's *me.*"

Her vision cleared. Landon was crouched over her, and he was wrapping her, Cush, and himself in a thin blanket of invisibility.

Ellis' hand hurt. Her palm was badly burned. Where the skin wasn't black, it had blistered. "Why are you here?"

"I got your call. I heard Errol attack you, and I came as soon as I could. We have to go. The woods are lousy with extremely unfriendly people who have guns."

Ellis cradled her burned hand, then pulled herself to a sitting position, only to gasp. "Dragonman!"

Landon steadied her. "It's okay. I brought a healing salve with me just in case."

Cush was perched on a log beside Dragonman. Because of his tattoos, it was hard to tell if he was still in shock, but his eyes were brighter.

"Can you carry him?" Ellis asked Cush.

Cush was dazed, but he nodded. He pulled his friend into his arms, then stood. He resembled a lost puppy.

Ellis finally noticed the dome of shadow magic. "Is this your work?" she asked her brother in amazement. She'd never seen Landon cast such a steady spell.

Her brother's lavender cheeks darkened in embarrassment. Ellis hadn't meant the question to be insulting, but it had wounded him. "Trissa's been helping me."

Ellis hissed. "Her potion was deadly."

"How much did you drink?"

Ellis' cheeks reddened. That potion was the only reason she was alive. "Um, all of it."

Landon whistled. "Mother Beneath. No wonder."

The ground felt spongy and unstable now that she was upright. The edges of her vision blurred, and the horizon tilted. She drew a deep breath and looked around to orient herself.

She blinked when she saw Cush. He was naked except for black combat boots and a pair of silk boxers printed with hearts.

Cush pointed at Landon. "He made me take my pants off."

"The lightsilk was too risky," Landon explained. "Can you walk?"

Ellis took a step, and the tree trunks went horizontal. She crouched until the dizziness subsided, but her next attempt was no better.

"No. Take Cush and go," she told Landon.

Landon snorted. "You're not the only person in the family who is allowed to play hero," he told her matter-of-factly, then ducked his head under Ellis' shoulder and put an arm around her waist. "Let's go."

They moved slowly since Ellis' limbs were sluggish and Cush was carrying Dragonman. They spoke little as they pushed through the vegetation. Ellis felt better the farther they went, and the helicopter's noise receding in the background helped.

"Thanks for coming," she blurted as Landon helped her over a deadfall at the top of a ravine. "You didn't have to."

"And miss my opportunity to lord this over you for years? Unlikely."

Cush joined them at the lip of the ravine and paused, breathing hard. "Do you and Shadow go to the same tattoo artist?"

Landon blinked. Ellis shot him a look. "Yes?" Landon ventured.

Cush nodded in satisfaction. "You could do a double act."

"I don't know if I'm cut out for circus life," Landon replied.

The moment of inattention doomed them. Landon screamed and toppled on his next step. Their envelope of shadow magic popped out of existence as he fell, and Ellis saw a silver string just below knee level.

A lightsilk trip line.

CHAPTER EIGHTEEN

Red and blue lights flashed between the tree trunks. A siren blasted Ellis' eardrums, which were raw from the gunfire and helicopter's whirring. Someone shouted.

Landon was on the ground, gripping his ankle. His face was twisted in agony. Ellis spied the thick dark welt on the purple skin of his ankle.

She hauled him upright, ignoring his cries of pain, then turned to Cush, who was still valiantly carrying Dragonman. "You have to hide."

"What? No! We have to *leave*." He shivered from fear and cold, and his piercings jingled.

"They're not looking for you. They're looking for us." Ellis ignored Landon's queasy look. "I saw a hollow under that deadfall a few hundred feet back. Hide there."

"Dragonman won't last much longer," Cush argued.

Ellis gritted her teeth as she wracked her brain to find a way out, but Landon beat her to it. "Give him the rest of this," he said. He offered Cush a small crystal vial full of a viscous rainbow-colored liquid.

Ellis recognized it. It was godmilk, the most powerful healing potion she knew about. She had once tried to make it and had wasted a full harvest of mushrooms.

"Pour some into his wound and make him drink the rest," Landon told Cush. "Do you understand?" The man nodded.

"Then go!" Ellis urged.

Landon handed the vial to Cush, who delicately took it between his teeth before disappearing into the forest.

It wasn't a moment too soon. A woman wearing a bulletproof vest and lightsilk jumpsuit like the other commandos emerged from the underbrush in front of Ellis and Landon, along with a tall, unarmored man. Errol.

"Freeze!" the woman barked. Ellis *swore* she'd heard her voice before.

Landon brandished his dagger, but Errol sighed. "Put it down, Lan." Even in the flashing lights, his eyes were red-rimmed. He looked tormented.

Ellis glared at him. "What have you *done?*"

Errol cringed. "I didn't have a choice."

"There's *always* a choice."

"You don't understand."

The woman's radio crackled. She lifted it to her mouth with the hand that was not holding her gun. "I have the MEC. Cuff him."

Errol pulled a pair of thick metal shackles from a pocket. Thick bands of steel connected them, and lightsilk lined the interior of each shackle. Errol barely flinched when his fingers brushed the gleaming fabric.

"One wrong move and I shoot you," the woman warned.

Errol handed the cuffs to Landon. "Put them on."

"Fuck, no!" Landon swiped at Errol with his dagger.

"Put them on, or I shoot the girl," the woman growled.

It came to Ellis in a flash. "*Liza!*" Charlie Morrissey's partner hadn't gone missing. She'd gone rogue.

Surprise flashed in the woman's eyes, which were bright behind the black wool mask that covered her face. Her finger twitched beside the trigger.

Landon dropped the dagger, and it thudded in the dirt. "Okay, I'm putting the cuffs on!"

Errol grabbed the moonsteel dagger and tested its edge, then looked at Ellis and Liza. "You two know each other?"

Liza's gaze was sharp but held a glimmer of empathy. "Take her into the woods," she told Errol. "They only know about one MEC. I'll deal with her after everyone leaves. I have questions."

Errol's eyes narrowed. "Questions? What kind of questions?"

"I can shoot her if you'd prefer," Liza spat.

"No, ma'am."

Liza pinned Ellis with a well-honed detective's stare. "What happened to the men from the compound? The one in the cabin with the piercings and the green guy in the field?"

Her voice cracked on the last word, and her eyes glistened in the flashing red lights. She regretted the possibility of collateral damage.

Ellis sent a prayer down to the Mother Beneath that Cush and Dragonman were safe, then muttered, "They're dead."

Errol growled, threw himself at Ellis, and wrapped his

hands around her neck. *"What did you do to them?"*

Ellis scrabbled at his fingers. Tears sprang to her eyes as the skin on her burned hand painfully cracked.

"Stop, or I shoot you both," Liza snapped. "I only need one of you alive."

Errol released Ellis but kept his fists clenched at his sides. "They were *good people.*"

Ellis coughed. "You should have thought about that before you called in commandos."

"Where are the bodies?" Liza's question was laced with fear and suspicion.

"Gone. I lost control of my magic while trying to escape and dissolved them." She hoped her exhaustion and pain would cover the lie.

"You *bitch.*" Errol wound up to punch Ellis in the face, but she blocked it with a kick.

A gunshot rang out. Ellis froze.

Liza lowered her rifle to point at the ground. She'd shot into the air. "No more of this bullshit. If you both want to live, take her into the woods *now.* I will come back for her later."

"I won't leave Landon!" Ellis protested.

Errol grabbed her arm, and the resulting flash of pain in her hand nearly made her pass out.

"There's no point," he told her through gritted teeth. "You have no idea what these people can do."

"I have *some* idea," Ellis shot back. She remembered the pool of blood under Captain Jericho's head.

"Save yourself, sis," Landon quietly said.

"No!"

Errol grumbled in exasperation, tightened his grip on

Ellis' arm, and dragged her off despite her protests as Liza marched Landon in the other direction.

Errol sank against a tree trunk. They hadn't gone far. Every instinct in her body told her to follow her brother, but Errol's grip hadn't loosened, and she couldn't fight a battalion of armed men without shadow magic.

She wished for another bottle of Trissa's potion. She didn't care if it killed her. It would be worth it to save Landon.

Burning hatred for Errol roiled in her stomach like a ball of lightsilk. The moment she'd gathered enough strength, Ellis would kill the traitorous, round-eared pile of guano with her bare hands.

"Landon *liked* you, you know," she told Errol. "He might have been the only drow who felt that way, but he did."

He winced and looked away, but Ellis didn't relent. "He thought you were brave for leaving the caverns. He looked up to you."

"He shouldn't have." The dark elf's breathing was ragged, and pain lined his face.

"No shit." Ellis let him sit with that, then asked, "Do you know who that woman is?"

"The one you called Liza? No. I can't recognize anyone behind the black masks, and they never send the same team twice. I think they're afraid someone might get attached."

"No need to worry about anyone getting attached to *you*." Errol's nails dug into her hand, and Ellis grimaced. "Why are you doing this? Money, or just for shits and giggles?"

When Errol finally replied, his voice was soft, and it

cracked. "They told me they could make me look human."

Ellis' eyebrows rose. "Really."

Errol stared at the ground. "I can't go home, so…"

"You could," she replied, but they both knew it was a lie.

"I like the open skies. It's fine. But I'll never have a real home if I look like this."

"You *had* a home. Cush and Dragonman liked you. Even Ophidia liked you until you betrayed them."

Errol's shoulders shook. "I didn't know the moon people would come with so many people and guns."

"Moon people? Is that what they're called?"

"I don't know. I call them the moon people because of the symbol they wear."

"Who are they?"

Errol shrugged. "All I know is that they're interested in drow. I'm not a complete monster. I thought they'd stop searching for entrances to the homestead if I gave you to them. They're getting close."

Ellis remembered the map of Los Angeles in Ron Jackson's safe deposit box. It had shown the approximate location of the Swallow's Nest circled in red.

"I saw them try to kidnap Landon once." Ellis recounted the incident with the van. "Did you do that too?"

Errol's eyes were dark pools of regret. "One of Landon's idiot friends was supposed to be at the bus stop that night, not him. Malvo, I think. They must have swapped places at the last minute."

"Why did you turn on your own people?"

Errol sighed. "The moon people showed up at the abandoned warehouse I was living in. They caught me in a lightsilk net and let me squirm for a while, then showed me a map of old exits from the homestead that had all caved in. They offered me freedom in exchange for information.

"They don't know where our main entrance is," he continued, "or they would already have attacked. I tried to throw them off the trail by pointing them at an old exit. I told them we only had supply caches here and most of us live up north, past the Canadian border.

"I don't think they believed me. They wanted to know where to find more drow. I told them there might be loners and stragglers around, and I eventually said I would help them find the others if they let me go."

"You betrayed us," Ellis accused.

Errol flinched. "No! I fed them bad information. I tried to warn Landon, but they watched this place and me all the time."

He laid the moonsteel dagger across his lap with the hand not gripping Ellis' wrist. "Like I said, I thought if I turned you over to them, they would stop looking for the homestead. You're not a real drow anyway."

Ellis' skin prickled with fury. She walked her good hand along the ground until she found a thick branch and wiggled it. The stick was loose.

Errol was wrong. She *was* a real drow. Moving to Los Angeles had taught her that. She was also strong, and she had been a powerful magician and hopefully would be again. In addition, she was a skilled mycologist. Not everyone in the Swallow's Nest accepted her, but if she died in this forest, they would never have the chance to see her for who she truly was.

"I'm more of a drow than you'll ever be," Ellis snarled.

She cracked the makeshift club over Errol's left hand,

the one holding her grandfather's moonsteel dagger. The wood splintered, but it turned two of Errol's fingers into a bloody pulp.

He released her wrist in shock, and his grip was weak when he slashed at her.

Ellis sprang to her feet and deflected the dagger thrust with a kick, but dizziness destabilized her aim, and the blade left a long, shallow cut on her calf. She ignored the pain and punched Errol in the shoulder.

His arm flopped, and he shrieked. He managed to keep his grip on the dagger, but as he tried to grab it with his other hand, Ellis kicked it to the ground.

Errol rolled his shoulder in a vain attempt to bring feeling back into his arm and glanced at the dagger. Ellis hoped he would dive for it since that would give her a badly needed opening. Instead, he squared up.

She had to remember that he was stronger than her, so without the element of surprise, she was outmatched. Errol had spent the past few years scrapping with biker gangs.

The bout wasn't pretty. Nobody would sing ballads about it. Ellis focused on hitting his injured arm and hand to distract him with pain. She outlasted him, and finally, he ran.

Ellis snatched the moonsteel dagger off the ground and toyed with the idea of hunting him down but decided he wasn't worth it. Instead, she followed the sound of water to a small creek. She scooped two handfuls into her mouth and splashed a third over her head. She couldn't help anyone if she passed out in the forest.

She struggled back to her feet and picked through the

vegetation toward the deadfall to which she'd directed Cush. She could hear the telltale jingle as she approached. Cush wasn't built for stealth.

"You can come out, Cush," she whispered.

He peeked out from his hiding spot and glittered under the moonlight. His face showed exhaustion and unflagging determination.

"Is Dragonman…" she ventured.

"Alive?" he finished. "Yeah."

"Good. I think all the people who attacked us are gone. Follow me, and if I shout, run back here. Got it?"

He nodded and turned back to retrieve his friend from the hollow.

Ellis didn't have the energy for further conversation. When Cush returned with Dragonman cradled in his arms, they plodded through the forest in silence.

The compound was dead quiet. The buildings were dark silhouettes against a darker night. Someone, probably the moon people, had cut off the power.

Ellis glanced at the ruins of the reptile house, then raised her hands above her head and clapped three times in case any of the snakes were still in the vicinity. She felt sorry for them outside on a cool night in an unfamiliar habitat.

Cush paused near the main house. "Should we look inside?"

Ellis grimaced. "No. They wouldn't have left anyone alive."

A rectangle of light shone in the parking area. The front windshield of a vehicle was illuminated, and something moved inside.

Ellis put a hand out to stop Cush. "Wait here," she whispered.

Cush, not eager to see any more action, obeyed as Ellis crept forward.

The movement resolved into a man clad in a shiny paisley shirt. Ellis' shoulders released their tension, and she grinned. "It's okay," she called to Cush.

Percy nearly jumped out of his skin when Ellis knocked on the car window, but when he recognized her face, he exploded out of the vehicle and wrapped her in a bear hug. "Ellis! *Ellis*, you had me so *worried!* I received some highly unusual reports from some highly unusual reptiles. They told me it was safe to drive up about fifteen minutes ago. What's going *on?*"

Percy was the only man on earth who would approach a field full of venomous snakes with enthusiasm. He looked up and started when Cush appeared behind Ellis, carrying Dragonman, but not much. His well of surprise was running low, like Ellis'.

Ellis eyed Percy's van, which had a boxy Space Age design she didn't recognize. "Where did you get a van?"

"It's a self-driving car," Percy proudly informed her. "I, uh, *encouraged* its processing unit to make a stop at our apartment. Now it's a me-driving car. It's a trick I've been wantin' to try for a good sweet minute, Ellis, but you were very insistent about staying off the radar."

Cush frowned at Percy. "You look familiar."

Ellis cut in. "No time for that. Dragonman needs a hospital." They could worry about Percy's fugitive status later.

"Who's Drag...oh." Percy cut himself off in mid-sentence as Cush stepped into the light from the open van door, then ran around to the back of the van and flung the doors open.

While he and Cush carefully situated the wounded man inside the van, Ellis looked around. Miraculously, Granny was still there.

They were here to take me, not my stuff.

Ellis reached for the front passenger door, but Percy stopped her. "That seat is currently occupied by several legless reptilian friends. While snakes are not inclined to hurt you out of spite, they've had a rough night, and I'd be surprised if anywhere closer than the San Diego Zoo stocks krait antivenin."

Ellis sucked in a breath as she peered through the dark glass at the sinuous shapes writhing in the front seat. At least twenty snakes were curled on the cushions, the dashboard, and around the door handles.

When she shuddered, Percy clapped her on the shoulder. "That fear is what keeps both you and the snake safe! Mother Nature produces a tidy solution once again."

Any desire to ride in the van disappeared. Ellis swung a leg over her bike and told Percy, "Drop Dragonman and Cush at the hospital, then meet me in the Bromeliad's parking garage. Tell the security guy you're Ellis' new spore supplier."

Percy took this at face value and hopped into the driver's seat. He nodded politely at the blanket of snakes within easy striking distance, then sped away into the night.

Mother Beneath. What had she gotten herself into?

CHAPTER NINETEEN

Dragonman would live, which was a tremendous relief. The doctors would have questions when they pulled a bullet out of him, questions they would undoubtedly delegate to the police, but he would live. Cush was crashing with a friend for the night. Ophidia was MIA.

Ellis had to rescue her brother. She had one lead on the people who had kidnapped them: the Bromeliad's basement, with its cave widow guards and lightsilk curtains. She was tempted to storm down immediately when she arrived, but Landon's life was at stake. He deserved all the help she could muster, even if she preferred to work alone.

Therefore, she called Charlie Morrissey.

She shivered in the basement while she waited for him to arrive, not because she was cold or because she was afraid to go in but because she anticipated learning that their relationship was damaged beyond repair. He might try to arrest her again, but Morrissey was very competent, and the authority signified by his badge could come in handy.

He was disgruntled when he stepped out of his car. He nodded curtly at Percy, then yelped in surprise when he saw the large snake coiled near the other man's feet. The king cobra had taken a shine to Percy.

"What the fuck, Ellis?" he exclaimed. "You need Animal Control, not homicide!"

"I might need both," she muttered.

Detective Morrissey offered no other greeting and approached with his arms crossed. If she wanted anything from him, she would have to pry it out.

"I found Liza," she told him.

"What? *Where?*" Charlie eyed Percy's van, then the king cobra. He swallowed hard, but Ellis suspected he'd fight the cobra without hesitation if he believed Liza was inside the van.

"Charlie, she wasn't kidnapped. I think she defected."

He frowned. "What do you mean?"

"It's a long story. I think she's with the organization that killed your captain. They were in Topanga Canyon tonight. They killed innocent people and kidnapped my brother."

Charlie shook his head. "You're lying. Liza flies as straight as an arrow. She would *never* get involved in anything like that."

"She might not know what she's gotten into. She let me go, so maybe she thought I could help." Ellis sketched out the night's events, although she left out what Errol had told her about the "moon people" and their interest in the drow.

Charlie crossed his arms again. "Why should I help you?"

"Because we're friends, and you do the right thing, even when it's hard," Ellis replied. "It would have been easy to let

Ron Jackson's crimes slide, but you didn't. This is *way* bigger than Ron Jackson."

He drew a deep breath, then slowly let it out. "Fine. I'll help you on one condition."

Ellis waited. She didn't dare breathe.

"If I don't like what I see tonight, I bring you in. You *and* Percy."

"Counteroffer. If you decide to arrest me, I won't fight you, but you don't take Percy."

She offered her hand, and when Morrissey shook it, his fingers were cold.

CHAPTER TWENTY

Percy had wanted to bring all of Ophidia's snakes to the Bromeliad. Venomous snakes weren't a bad choice for the job since they could investigate small spaces and hold their own against cave widows. Percy also insisted that they were grateful to him for rescuing them from the sideshow performers' property, and they wanted to help.

"*I'm* the one who freed them," Ellis had grumbled.

"Flinging them unprotected into the night is hardly freedom," Percy had admonished.

In the end, Percy decided that only the king cobra would accompany them. It slithered behind Percy like a show dog.

Charlie nearly puked when Ellis told him the snake was coming along for the ride. "Motherfucking snakes in a motherfucking basement," he whispered.

Percy noticed the detective's frozen posture and wide pupils. He went to the van and retrieved the trident they'd made for Ellis. He gently removed a neon-green snake from the tines, replaced the reptile in the van, and handed the trident to Charlie. "This is for mental comfort *only*. Don't poke my friend for no reason."

Charlie pointed the trident at the cobra. "I don't want it behind me."

Ellis couldn't agree more. "Lead the way," she told Percy, and the weird group left the parking garage with a king cobra as the vanguard.

They encountered only one person in the halls. The janitor took one look at the cobra, crossed himself, and walked into a supply closet. The lock snicked as they walked past.

At the elevator, Ellis fished the little gold key out of her pocket. This was the point of no return, except that Charlie was standing outside the elevator car and staring at the king cobra, which had curled into a knot in a corner.

"I will not ride an elevator with a ten-foot-long poisonous snake," he flatly stated.

Again, Ellis couldn't blame him. She promised she'd be back in a minute.

She was antsy every second the elevator doors were closed. The janitor could have called Amelia, Animal Control, or the UCLA herpetology department. Hell, Charlie could have decided she was loony and left.

He was right where she'd left him when the door opened.

He checked the elevator thoroughly before walking in. "You trust that unhinged little bank robber an awful lot," he muttered.

"He deserves it."

"That's how I feel about Liza." Charlie sounded sad. "I trust her as much as I've ever trusted anyone."

Ellis stepped into the far corner of the elevator car to avoid the deep suspicion in his eyes. "They killed innocent people in Topanga."

"You don't know that they were innocent," Charlie replied. "They could have been running drugs up there or worse. You may not have all the information." He wasn't convincing.

"You still think we can rescue her," Ellis stated.

Charlie just stewed until the elevator doors opened, then brandished his trident as he stepped out.

Percy was still there, but his face was the color of the walls, and he was staring into a vent. Even with her excellent night vision, Ellis could barely see the segmented eyes of the cave widow glittering in the darkness where she crouched at the edge of the flashing red light.

Percy swayed in time with the eerie tone pulsing from the speakers affixed under the vents. "When you asked me about spiders…"

"Will they be a problem?" she asked.

"We can deal with a few spiders," Charlie scoffed. Ellis suspected he'd change his tune after he saw a cave widow for the first time.

Percy looked them all in the eye, including the cobra. "Let me be clear. If you see anything with more than six legs, you kill it dead as can be. No questions."

Charlie snorted. "No problem. My shoes have thick soles."

"I'm serious," Percy admonished.

He touched the king cobra's tail, which made Ellis wince in anticipation, but it just slithered ahead of him. Ellis felt the gazes of the cave widows in the vents as they walked, but none emerged to block their passage. The stairs to sub-basement four were empty as well.

They gathered in the small space beyond the door at the bottom of the stairwell. Ellis gulped as she gazed at the lightsilk curtains. They would burn like a shadowless sun. She was jealous of the cobra, which could slide under the dangling threads.

Charlie grabbed a handful of lightsilk and ran his thumb over the threads. "This is the stuff you're...allergic to, isn't it?"

"Yes."

"What'll happen if you touch it?"

"It'll hurt like hell."

"What about your special skills?"

Ellis sighed. "They're so depleted that it won't matter."

She wished she hadn't been so stupid as to chug the entire bottle of shadow potion. Even a few drops would have helped her now.

Charlie was scowling at the lightsilk as though Ellis had invited him to swim with alligators. "You're sure it won't hurt us?"

"No, just me. Because of my...special skills."

Percy pointed at Charlie's trident. "Use your stick. We'll keep as much of it off you as we can, Ellis."

Charlie gripped the skein of silk threads in a way that made Ellis think he was tempted to rip off a hank, tie her up, and haul her to the station. He ultimately dropped them and shook his head.

He stared at the half-moon symbol on the far wall and murmured, "Something about that feels wrong." Then, he swept a swath of threads aside with his trident to create a tunnel for Ellis to step through.

Charlie and Percy took turns moving the lightsilk aside. Ellis was embarrassed, feeling like spoiled royalty, until a strand slipped and drifted across her face.

Ellis' breath caught in her throat as the line of fire seared her skin. She clapped her hand to her cheek and felt the welt rising.

Charlie stopped ahead of her. "What the *fuck?*"

Percy, who was beside her, was holding a bunch of lightsilk aside, and his arm twitched when he saw two cave widows drop from open vents at the end of the hallway. Ellis hadn't seen the dark openings through the glittering curtains.

"*Stop!*" Percy bellowed. The command had a feral, animalistic edge that made her sweat in the chill air. Percy was psychically communicating with the spiders. The power that allowed the mind-to-mind connection felt like static.

"Remember what I said," Percy whispered. It was a warning to the spiders and a reminder to Ellis.

A spider fixed her with its gaze. Its eyes were sparkling, segmented kaleidoscopes. Colors danced within them like reflections in an onyx mirror. She could stare at them all day.

The spider jumped.

Ellis was drowning in the swirling colors of the spider's hypnotic gaze, and Charlie was frozen where he stood. Percy dropped the lightsilk and ran past Ellis.

The strands landed on Ellis in a rope an inch thick that split and spread as it fell. Her vision went black when they drifted across her eyelids, but she shielded her face with her forearms and sprinted forward. It was absurd and dangerous, but there was no turning back.

Percy jerked the trident out of Charlie's hand and flung it at the nearest spider with sure aim. The spider hissed, and viscous black liquid poured from its mouth. Its eight legs jerked as it collapsed.

Ellis hit the growing pool of spider guts, and her foot went out from under her. She grabbed the jutting trident to stay upright but slid through the remaining lightsilk strands at speed and slammed into the painted half-moon logo.

She dropped to the floor. The pain from the lightsilk had dimmed enough that she realized she was face-to-face with the king cobra.

"Who's a good boy?" Ellis weakly ventured.

The snake hissed. Its head was at least three feet off the ground. It swayed, then struck. Its short fangs were white streaks as its thick body sailed past her and it bit into the second cave widow's abdomen.

The spider reared, its talon-tipped front legs pointing at the cobra. Ellis plunged her grandfather's moonsteel dagger into the spider's head.

Percy ran toward them with Charlie at his heels. "Get away from it," he hissed.

Ellis shied back. When Percy pulled the cobra back, she realized he'd been warning the snake away from the spider. Even dead, he seemed terrified of the arachnid. She'd never have pegged him for an arachnophobe, but stranger things had happened.

Ellis panted. Puffy red welts striped her arms, and she

doubted her face looked much better. "Thanks for the concern," she grumbled.

When he was satisfied that the cobra was far enough away, Percy seized the makeshift trident and plunged it into the spider's head and abdomen. Then he kicked the body off the tines. His fingers were bone-white around the wooden handle, and tears glistened in his eyes.

"Percy?" Ellis cautiously asked.

He didn't move. His lips trembled, and he fell to his knees beside the spider's wrecked corpse.

Percy loved all animals. Not just dogs and cats, but diseased pigeons and sewer rats and even king cobras. Bugs were harder to understand, but he loved them, too. He was not an arachnophobe. Something wasn't right.

"Have you ever run across pure evil, Ellis?" Percy's voice was a monotone.

The commandos who had taken the Topanga Canyon compound had been efficient and brutal. They had been well-organized, and they had kidnapped her brother, but had they been *evil*?

"I don't know," she admitted. "Are you all right?"

He shook his head. "That spider was evil. Animals aren't evil. Violent, yes. Self-interested, but animals do not walk in the black places in the soul. *People* do the truly terrible things."

"No lie there," Charlie muttered. He'd seen the worst of it.

"I've only ever known one person who could turn an animal this bad."

"Who?"

Footsteps echoed from around the corner, cutting off

Percy's reply. Morrissey unholstered his gun in record time.

"The video made *no* sense. It looked like a goddamn snake—" The man and a woman who came around the corner froze. Given the tableau of Percy and his makeshift trident, Ellis looking like she'd been in a cage match, an armed LAPD detective, and a king cobra, that did not surprise Ellis.

"LAPD! Freeze!" Charlie commanded.

Liza gasped. *"Charlie?"* Her automatic rifle remained leveled at Charlie's torso despite her recognition. Her gaze slid to Ellis. *"You.* Did you disable our inside source, or did he defect?"

"Inside source?"

Liza huffed. "The purple guy."

"His name's Errol."

"We don't use names."

"Agent L, you know this guy?" The man beside Liza nodded at Morrissey. Ellis couldn't tell if he had been in the forest. He was carrying a handgun rather than a rifle, and when he noticed the cobra, he didn't wait for Liza to respond before pointing his sidearm at the big snake and pulling the trigger.

Percy shouted, "No!" and leaped forward. He wasn't faster than a bullet, but fortunately, the gunman missed. The bullet dented the tile a heartbeat before Percy grabbed the cobra's neck.

He whispered something to the snake, and after it stopped thrashing, he wound the cobra around his neck like a scarf. The man in black shifted his target to Percy's center of mass. The hacker didn't seem bothered. "He's not a threat."

Liza blinked. "*He* is a fast-striking venomous snake."

"That's correct." Percy frowned.

"Release my brother, and no one gets hurt," Ellis told the two soldiers.

Liza ignored her. "You're working with the vigilante?" she asked Charlie. She sounded disappointed.

Ellis scowled. *I'll show you disappointed. I'll disappoint your face with my boot.*

"We both have some explaining to do," Charlie evenly replied.

Her eyebrows shot up. "Don't give me that 'we're the same' bullshit. You went rogue."

"And you didn't?"

"Show him the badge, Agent M," Liza ordered.

Agent M warily eyed the king cobra as he shuffled forward, pulled a bright brass circle from his pocket, and flashed it at them. It showed the half-moon symbol in its two concentric circles and had three letters at the top that stood out in sharp relief, DRI.

"What's the DRI?" Charlie asked.

"That's classified," Agent M replied.

Charlie grunted in disgust. "In that case, I work for the FU."

Agent M blinked in confusion. "The Federal Unit of..."

"*No*, for God's... Never mind."

Liza glared at Charlie. "Does this look like some ragtag militia to you? Do you think I would *join* a ragtag militia?"

Morrissey froze. He respected his partner, which might

be enough to convince him this place was a legitimate government agency. Ellis couldn't let that happen.

"You killed innocent people," she cut in.

"War is hell," Liza retorted, but she sounded uncertain.

"Who are you at war with?" Charlie demanded.

"That's classified," Agent M stated curtly.

"Put the gun down, Charlie, and we'll go somewhere we can talk." Liza spoke with forced feminine softness, and Ellis trusted it zero percent.

When Liza tentatively stepped forward, Charlie barked, "Stop!" She did, and he challenged her with, "If this is a real government agency, how much paperwork do you have to do this week?"

"That's classified," Agent M repeated.

Charlie threw the guy a disgusted look. "Can you teach this guy a second phrase while you're at it, Liza?"

Liza rolled her eyes. "Well, for starters, M here discharged his gun at that snake, so that's Form—"

Agent M cut her off with a sharp shake of his head, and she sighed. "That's one form. Plus, this counts as a security incident, which means an incident report. Each eight-legged guard requires a property destruction memo—"

Percy's hackles rose, but he didn't argue. Ellis suspected it had to do with his feelings about the spiders being evil.

"And if we want to move spiders from the training pens, we gotta do a requisition request," Liza finished.

"*Training pens?*" Percy's objections to the evil spiders apparently didn't extend to his horror about treating animals as property. His agitation jostled the king cobra, whose mouth opened to reveal its fangs.

Agent M shot Liza a sharp look. Ellis guessed that the

training pens were equally classified. Then he stared at Percy. "You look familiar."

Liza let out a sharp bark of laughter. "He's the most-wanted bank robber in the country. Of course, he looks familiar."

"No, that's not it." Agent M shook his head to clear it, then peered at Percy again.

Liza raised her voice. "If I have to shoot you, that's another weapon discharge form, a mortality report, and a base safety incident form. I'd also have to book time in Organics Disposal." Her expression turned queasy.

Ellis had fought a lot of criminals lately. She didn't like much about them, but they didn't bother disguising their misdeeds with official-sounding language.

"Is it hard to book time in Organics Disposal?" Ellis coldly asked. "Is that a busy department?"

Liza cringed.

Agent M loomed over Charlie. "If you don't put that gun down, you'll have plenty of personal experience with Organics Disposal."

"This place is legit, Charlie," Liza softly said. "I have health insurance and dental. I even have pet insurance for Boomerang."

Percy whistled appreciatively.

"They also kidnapped my brother," Ellis reminded her companions.

Liza frowned. "Your brother?"

"Is she talking about the MEC? How is that possible?" Agent M's face went pale, and he trained the gun on Ellis. His gaze traveled over the red welts, and his eyes narrowed.

Liza replied, "I don't know, but she's dangerous. That's for sure."

"Hell, yeah, I am." Ellis would show them how dangerous she was when the gun was no longer pointing at her chest.

"You can't trust her, Charlie," Liza insisted. "Before you became obsessed with her, you were a good cop."

Charlie's shoulders slumped. "I still am."

"You've been sneaking around and associating with fugitives. Mixed up in nasty business."

"That doesn't make me a bad cop. Things have gotten complicated."

"Let me make them simple again. Join us. I'll explain everything. All you have to do is put down the gun."

The barrel dropped half an inch. Ellis shouted, "*Charlie, no!*"

It was too late. Detective Morrissey spun and leveled his gun at Ellis.

Liza's face glowed with relief, although Agent M remained uncertain. He kept his gun pointed at Charlie's back until Liza shook her head, at which point he sighed and holstered it. Then, he pulled a long metal tube from a leather sheath on his belt.

Ellis was unable to divine the tube's purpose until he raised it to his lips and a dart hit her in the neck. The lines of the hallway went fuzzy. She slumped on a tile floor that felt like a down mattress and floated into a cloudy white haze.

CHAPTER TWENTY-ONE

Ellis' eyes fluttered open. She hurt *badly*. Every muscle ached, every joint creaked, and when she sat up, her vision blurred.

She put her hands on her knees to regain her balance. The fabric under her fingers was rough. A quick check at her back confirmed that it was a hospital gown tied with two thin cords.

Ellis was on a thin mattress on a metal floor in an unusual cell. Thick metal bars supported a circular concrete slab ten feet over her head, and creamy opaque lightsilk hung around the outside. A punishingly bright floodlight was tied to a bar. Ellis would have smashed it, but it had a lightsilk cover. The whole thing felt like a covered birdcage.

Standing up seemed impossible, so Ellis scooted along the perimeter of the cell and hunted for gaps in the light-silk. She only found a Velcro seam behind the cell's door, which was padlocked shut.

She reached through the bars and ran her fingers over

the padlock. It was manageable. She could pick it in her sleep.

Ellis reached for her moonsteel lockpicks and gasped when she realized her hair had been cropped short. *I will kill those assholes.*

She attempted to lever the nearest bar out of the concrete slab but had no luck. She was strong, but not *that* strong. She tested each bar in turn, but none budged.

Ellis flopped on the mattress and stared at the ceiling. She could tunnel through the concrete ceiling if she had time and equipment or her shadow magic, but she had neither.

Her burned hand had been cleaned and wrapped in a loose bandage, and a rubber bowl of water was beside her bed. Ellis sniffed it, then enthusiastically drank. Why would they poison her? They could have killed her in her sleep if that was what they wanted.

She wondered if she could turn the bowl into a weapon, but the sides were flexible and deformed in her hands.

She put it down beside an identical bowl full of round pellets. Ellis plucked one from the pile. The texture and smell reminded her of dog food, and she wasn't hungry enough to eat that. Not yet, anyway.

The only other item in the room was a third rubber bowl. Ellis could guess its function.

"Hello!" Ellis called. "Is anyone there? Can I have some tacos?"

A man outside the lightsilk admonished, "No talking!"

Like that'll stop me. "Where's Percy? I want to talk to Charlie!"

"MECs don't talk!" The man wasn't agitated, just insistent.

Ellis scooted in his direction. As she opened her mouth to remark upon his crazy statement, an electric shock hummed through the metal floor and into her. Her muscles contracted, and she went rigid.

The hum ceased, and Ellis collapsed. Through the ringing in her ears, the man repeated, "No talking."

Okay, no talking. Ellis crawled back to her mattress and curled up. She would have to get answers another way.

When her skin stopped tingling, Ellis cupped her hands together and reached for the darkness in the gap between her palms. For the first time in her life, she couldn't sense the shadow magic.

It wasn't that she couldn't *use* it, as it had felt after the lightsilk confetti attack. It was as though the magic had vanished from the universe.

Ellis let her hands fall to the bed. Salty tears streaked down her face and burned where they crossed the welts left by the lightsilk.

She would try again in a few hours. In the meantime, she closed her eyes and listened.

Footsteps echoed off the walls, far enough away that Ellis sensed she was in a large room. The footsteps paused, followed by the distinctive rip of Velcro parting. That was good since it meant two things: one, she wasn't the only prisoner, and two, someone would eventually visit her. Every delivery of water or food pellets was an opportunity to learn more or even escape.

Ellis' stomach grumbled. She ignored it, and it grumbled again. She hadn't eaten since before Landon's foam-sword fighting event.

She sat up and grudgingly retrieved the rubber bowl of food. She rolled a pellet between her fingers. It was dry. She sipped more water and popped the pellet into her mouth.

It tasted better than it smelled, which was to say, it didn't taste like anything. Were they making Landon eat this, too? She would kill for some mushroom stew.

Ellis slowly chewed pellets until her stomach stopped complaining. She left the remainder in the bowl and set it back on the floor, then drained her water bowl and meditatively squished it.

Hang on a minute. Ellis' grip tightened on the rubber. Rubber was an insulating material. It could protect her from electrical shocks.

Ellis dumped the pellets on the floor beside her bed and swept them into a neat pile, then turned the bowl over and placed it on the floor. She did the same thing with the still-empty third bowl.

She stood and tentatively stepped onto the first bowl. It squashed, but she could stand on it. She grinned and put her other foot on the second bowl.

"Hey, buddy! How about a room service menu?" Ellis called. She tried to sound casual, but her voice trembled.

"No *talking*!" The man outside sounded incredulous. The faint electric hum returned, and the floor vibrated, but this time, it didn't hurt.

Ellis erupted into nervous laughter. "Is that the best you've got? Give me more juice, juice man!" The hum got louder, but Ellis was insulated on her rubber archipelago.

"Landon!" Ellis yelled, "If you're out there, I'm here, and I'm alive!"

The hum stopped. The Velcro seam of the lightsilk ripped open, and her guard peered in. He was in his fifties, with heavy jowls and expressionless eyes.

Ellis looked past him into the room beyond. It was bigger than she'd expected. She saw a wall maybe a hundred feet away.

"What are you doing? Get off those," he scolded, but his eyes were wide. Something about her surprised him. His gaze traveled from her face to her ears, uncovered by her unwelcome pixie cut.

Ellis knew that look. She had grown up with people who stared at her ears like that. He had expected her to be a drow, and when he saw that she wasn't, he was uncomfortable.

Rage as powerful as an electric current rushed through Ellis. If she had been purple with pointed ears, he would have thought this horrible treatment was fine and even appropriate.

She had to keep her anger in check. This man's hesitation was an opportunity. He didn't need to know she was a drow until she was snapping his neck.

Ellis batted her eyelashes. "Please, you have to help me! There's been a mistake!" She pitched her voice high. In her experience, the higher she made her voice, the less prepared men were when she kicked them in the face.

The lightsilk shifted as the guard anxiously glanced over his shoulder, afraid that he was losing control. Through the gap, she saw another tent twenty feet from hers, and she heard footsteps on metal. The other prisoner was listening.

"I'm hungry," Ellis pleaded. She clutched her stomach for effect.

The guard dumbly pointed at the loose pile of pellets near Ellis' bed. His face was awash with embarrassment.

Ellis did her best rich-lady impression and whined, "That's not *food!*" She'd heard so many Bromeliad patrons complain that she could mimic the attitude in her sleep.

The guard grimaced. He agreed with her. His fingers drifted over the gun at his waist, and he retrieved a candy bar from his back pocket. He offered it to her. "Here."

Ellis batted her eyelashes again and smiled as pathetically as she could. She stepped up to the bars and reached through them. She didn't have to fake the tremble in her hand.

I'm about to make the king cobra the second-fastest striker in the world.

Ellis pushed off her back foot, grabbed the guard's neck, and drove her knee into his groin. She choked off his attempt at a scream, and when he reached up to pull her fingers away, she slipped her other hand through the bars and grabbed his gun, wincing as her injured palm curled around the metal.

The guard thrashed, but Ellis waited until he stopped moving. His pulse was faint under her fingers. He was only unconscious.

Someone she couldn't see shouted, probably a guard at the other end of the chamber. She had to move fast.

Ellis held the guard against the bars and steeled herself to pick his lightsilk pockets. Her skin burned where it brushed the fabric, but she methodically worked her way down one leg and up the other.

No keys, but she found a familiar confetti gun and a latched case that held two small syringes full of a liquid that shimmered in the light. The sickening pink hue made Ellis uneasy. It felt like something Tower of London Barbie would use.

Heavy footsteps approached at a run, and someone yanked the lightsilk off her cage.

Ellis gaped. The room she was in could hold at least two football fields, and fifty or more of the lightsilk-covered cells stretched toward the walls in neat rows. It was a vast underground tent prison.

One guard had reached her cell, and three others were approaching. The one who had removed the lightsilk paused when he saw Ellis' gun. His gaze darted to his unconscious brother-in-arms under the curtain, and he dove for a red button on a free-standing console.

Ellis suspected she knew what the button did and leaped for her rubber "shoes." She misjudged her leap, accidentally kicked one bowl aside instead of landing on it, and wobbled on one foot as the shock shot through the metal floor.

"She killed her guard!" the man called. He reached for his gun. Ellis fired, but her bullet glanced off one of the bars.

The three other guards caught up. One pulled the unconscious guard out from under the lightsilk and checked his vitals. "He's alive!" Ellis noticed she wasn't wearing lightsilk.

The guard at whom she'd fired leveled his pistol at Ellis'

face, but another guard grabbed his arm. "This one's do-not-kill, remember?" the third guard urged.

"I don't give a shit if she's the reincarnation of Mother Teresa. Take her down."

"Put down the gun," the other man pleaded. His eyes were wide. He was afraid of his bosses, and Ellis couldn't blame him.

"Bring me my brother," Ellis replied.

The guard frowned. "Brother? I thought we only brought in purples this week. Is she a shapeshifter?"

Ellis snorted. She couldn't help it.

The first guard scowled. "What she *is* is dead."

Ellis shifted to put her heart behind a bar, and he tracked her with the barrel of his gun.

The medic who had dragged away Ellis' initial guard returned. She held a gun with a silencer. Ellis swallowed hard. She couldn't block both lines of sight.

The medic fired at the guard with the gun, hitting him in the gap between his helmet and body armor. A liquid gurgle followed the compressed *ping*, and he collapsed.

The second guard started. "What the—" The medic shot him in the neck too, and blood splashed on the metal at Ellis' feet.

The woman pushed the red button. "The floor's safe now."

Ellis was still standing on one foot. She tapped the metal with a toe and relaxed when she found it was inert.

The woman produced a key from a pocket and unlocked Ellis' cell. "Help me pull them inside."

They dragged the two dead and one unconscious

guards into the cage. Ellis removed their earpieces, then her savior locked the door and re-hung the lightsilk.

Landon was here somewhere. Ellis opened her mouth to call for him, but the woman covered her mouth.

"I need to find my brother," Ellis whispered.

"He's not here," the woman curtly informed her. "Guards will come if you scream."

The woman pointed her gun at Ellis' guts, and she froze. "What…"

"I won't shoot you, but I need to make it look real. Come on."

Ellis cast her gaze over the tents in despair as they walked. There were too many. Even if Landon was here, the whole facility would have mobilized by the time she found him. Going with the other woman was Ellis' best chance to live long enough to find him.

"Put your arms behind your back," the woman hissed. Ellis obeyed.

Two guards flanked the exit, their faces uncovered. One put up a hand and asked, "What's going on, soldier?"

"Boss wants her," Ellis' captor replied.

"It's not on the schedule."

"I have my orders. If you wanna cause a twenty-minute delay, that's on you."

The guard eyed them. His gaze lingered on Ellis' rounded ears, and she wanted to spit in his face.

He opened the door, revealing another corridor with cream-colored walls and a concrete floor. Ellis could be ten feet from where she'd been captured. She couldn't tell.

The woman pulled her along. Ellis' hospital gown fluttered behind her, but this was not the time to be self-conscious.

"Are you taking me to Landon? Where's Percy?" she hissed.

"Who's Percy?"

"The guy with the snake."

The woman shook her head. "We don't have time."

Ellis stopped dead. "I won't leave without them."

The woman tugged Ellis' arm, but she used every ounce of her drow strength to stand like a rock. The woman raised her gun. "One way or another, you *will* come with me."

It was a bluff, and Ellis knew it. She strode back down the hall.

The woman caught up and grabbed her arm again. "Stop! Everyone else is in the intake lab, except maybe the snake. I can take you there, but it won't be easy."

"I don't care. I won't leave them here."

"Okay. This way, then. Stay in front of me."

The guard marched her down the corridor. Ellis was lost after a handful of turns. White light filled the halls, and they all looked the same.

They passed another pair of guards, who looked curiously at Ellis and nodded at her guard but said nothing.

Finally, the woman stopped and pointed up. "Here."

Ellis stumbled back. The woman was pointing at one of the vents that allowed the cave widows to move through the building. "No way."

The woman fished in a pocket and came out with a small round device that resembled Percy's kitchen timer.

"This is a flash beacon. It'll keep the spiders away long enough for us to get where we need to go."

"To the lab?"

"Yeah. To the lab. The vent goes back twenty feet to an access tunnel. That's where we're headed."

"Okay." Ellis straightened. She could do this. She would fight a thousand spiders for Percy and her brother.

"Boost me up."

Ellis cupped her hands and helped the woman up to the vent, and she slithered in on her elbows. Apparently, she knew that Ellis could climb in without help, which was interesting.

Who *was* this woman? Was she helping Ellis because she looked human? That didn't seem right.

The anti-spider beacon twanged in the vent, muffled by the woman's body. Ellis hopped up and hauled herself into the vent, which was roomier than it looked. Even crawling on her elbows, her head only occasionally brushed the top.

The red flashes reflected hypnotically off the vent's walls. Spider webs hung in the corners. The woman had pushed through most of them, but some strands remained, and they clung to Ellis' skin.

The twenty feet passed quickly, and the woman dropped out of sight with a thump of boots on concrete. Ellis followed and stuck her head into a circular shaft. A narrow ledge circled the opening, and a ladder stretched away in both directions. The woman was waiting on the ladder above.

Ellis heard skittering in the shaft above them. Cave widows were disappearing into vents, chased away by the beacon.

"Come on. We only have a few more minutes," the woman urged.

She began climbing, and Ellis followed. She wondered how far they'd have to go. She was accustomed to climbing hundred-foot buildings, so this shouldn't be too hard.

She was wrong.

Within minutes, her forearms ached, and the beacon's tone and lights were fading. Ellis kept her gaze fixed on the darkness beyond her rescuer, and a hatch eventually swam into view. The beacon died three rungs later.

"*Move!*" the woman shouted.

The small device bounced off Ellis' head. She watched it ricochet off the shaft's wall and disappear. In the darkness below her feet, compound eyes glittered, and the clatter of talons on metal and concrete echoed up to her.

Ellis scrambled up the ladder. Ahead of her, the woman grunted as she shouldered the hatch open with a metallic creak. Light poured in, blinding Ellis, and the woman pulled her out of the tunnel as the spiders hissed at the searing intrusion.

The heavy metal lid crashed shut, severing a spider's leg with a crunch. An electronic lock clicked as it latched.

Ellis blinked to clear the bright spots from her vision. She heard birds chirping and children yelling and laughing.

This wasn't a lab. It was a park.

Ellis spun on the woman. "*Where the hell are we?*"

The woman, still wearing her opaque helmet, was doubled over, catching her breath. "I had to get you out. You wouldn't have come if I'd told you the truth."

A desperate scream scraped Ellis' throat raw, and she flung herself at the hatch from which they had emerged. It had no handle, and the seams were too thin for her fingernails to find purchase. She scrabbled at it in vain.

"It won't open from the outside," the woman wearily told her.

"You made me leave them behind!" Ellis tackled her, prepared to claw the woman's eyes out, but her cries died in her throat when she pulled off the woman's helmet.

Even though her blonde hair was streaked with gray and plastered to her head, and tears blurred her ice-blue eyes, her face was unmistakable.

It was Claire Burton.

Ellis tried to say, "Mom," but it came out as a gurgle.

Her mother sadly smiled. "Hello, Ellis."

Ellis' brain stuttered. She wanted to scream, fight, shake answers out of her mother, cry, or maybe faint. She just whimpered.

"It's good to see you, sweetheart. Would you mind letting me up? You're crushing me."

Ellis rolled off, lay on her back in the grass, and allowed the clouds to slip past. She finally said, "Ron Jackson told me he killed you."

Warm fingers gripped her uninjured hand. "Ron Jackson doesn't have a truthful bone in his worm-shit body."

Ellis laughed. The sound was high and frantic. She was losing control. "What... Why..." She couldn't pick a question. "We have to save Landon."

Claire bit her lip. "It never occurred to me that you might have a brother," she confessed. "I didn't even know you were alive. When we found your blood on that police captain's wall, I feared the worst."

"What? You found my *blood?"*

"I promise I'll explain everything. We'll also rescue your brother and your snake friend, although I can't promise the safety of that cobra." Claire shivered. "But we can't do it alone. There are too many guards. We need help."

Ellis clenched her teeth. "I don't care how many people I have to fight."

"You *should* care. They have safesilk nets, guns, and a *lot* of really big spiders."

"You call it 'safesilk?'"

Claire put a fingertip on a welt on Ellis' arm. Although the touch was gentle, it burst a blister, and Ellis winced. Claire snatched her hand away. "We'll clean you up, and then we'll go to the one person who can help us."

"Charlie betrayed me."

"The policeman did, yes, but that's not who I meant." Claire closed her eyes, then whispered, "Ellis, you need to take me to your father."

THE STORY CONTINUES

The story continues with The Chronicles of Shadow Bourne book four, coming soon to Amazon and Kindle Unlimited.

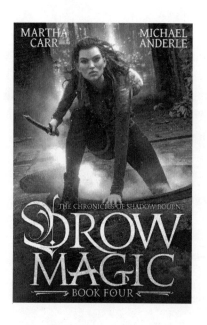

Get sneak peeks, exclusive giveaways, behind the scenes content, and more. PLUS you'll be notified of special **one day only fan pricing** on new releases.

Sign up today to get free stories.

Visit: https://marthacarr.com/read-free-stories/

AUTHOR NOTES - MARTHA CARR

WRITTEN JANUARY 22, 2024

I've started a project answering questions for my son about my life. I realized after last year's fifth round of cancer, and then chemo this time that he was expecting me to die sooner rather than later. It's been a lot for him to deal with and there isn't much I can do to make it better, except tell him stories that I can leave behind – eventually. Hopefully, a long time from now. I'm going to let you guys listen in as well.

My author notes for this year are going to be answers to questions and all of you can get to know me better, too. Maybe inspire, maybe give you a laugh along the way.

Today's question is: What is the best trip you've ever taken?

One of the best trips I've ever taken was with you to the west coast of Ireland a few years back. I remember I rented what the Irish apparently think of as a bigger car, the size of a compact here, that was an automatic. I bring that up because right out of the parking lot, the driving was hairy. Fortunately for both of us, you did all the driving.

First off, it was on the wrong side of the road. Second, there is a major highway with beautiful broad lanes but for some reason we kept choosing the back roads.

Those roads were narrow with a rock wall on one side and generally a cliff or an ocean or some body of water on the other side. Occasionally there were sheep scattered here and there like we were in a video game and had reached the next level where the goal is to avoid the bored sheep. Those miniature wooly beings were completely unafraid of both tourist buses or tourist drivers. I think they had a death wish.

Just for fun, there was the occasional switchback, a turn that is worse than a ninety-degree angle and what I love about you is that you felt obligated to take those steep turns at the posted speed. Did I mention the tour buses that took up just a touch over their lane, barreling down the road in the opposite direction.

Then, for the last piece the GPS immediately directed us to the middle of a cow pasture (not a road), that we dutifully took and got to the middle, looking around, and you said, "I don't think this is a road." The cows barely stopped munching on grass as you turned the rental car around on a rocky hill and casually commented, "These cars can really take it."

We got to our first roundabout and you looked at me, already a little worn out from driving, and said, "I'm just going to go around for a while." I completely understood.

We had been in the country less than an hour.

But, once we got to the Cliffs of Mohr and saw how many Americans had dented their rental cars, we felt a lot better about our odds.

The cliffs were amazing because it was the first time in a very long time that I had stood anywhere and couldn't hear a single man-made sound. No whirring or humming or buzzing or dinging. Nothing but the wind coming off the ocean far below. To add to the mystique, there was a stone wall dating back hundreds of years with a path that had been taken by generations for hundreds of years to pass from one village to another. It's a cool thing to walk even part of the path, imagining the lives of our ancestors who came before us.

In Lisdoonvarna I remember all the hubbub was about the annual singles weekend where hundreds showed up hoping to find their honey. There were signs everywhere about it and apparently the hotels would sell out and the streets would be packed with the ever hopefuls. We heard all kinds of stories about how successful it was.

Remember the Irish gypsy who owned the B&B we stayed at in another coastal town? She only accepted cash to stay there and sang every morning while guests ate breakfast. Out back I could see all her laundry hanging on the line.

Then there was Kylemore Abbey in Connemara that still houses nuns and has one of the most beautiful Victorian gardens. I loved wandering around there imagining having a garden anything like that someday. The cool thing is I actually accomplished it. My version at least.

I wish I could remember where we were when we walked that long dirt path that had oak trees that towered over us with roots so large they rose up to greet us almost to our height. It was like an enchanted forest. I think that was the place that had the small restaurant we accidentally found with herbs and vegetables from the garden just outside their door.

Or when we went to catch the tour boat in Killary Harbour just outside of Connemara to get a tour of the only fjord on the west coast. We just missed one boat and had almost two hours to wait for the next one. But like the most of the trip, we got lucky. There was a sole food truck that had just opened with a chef serving fresh mussels. We were her first customers ever and she gave us far too many.

We sat by the water at a small table slowly eating mussels, quietly listening to the sound of the water lapping against the small pier.

Eventually, the boat came back and we got on, full and happy, and rode down the fjord listening to the history of the area. That was close to where our ancestor, Frances Dean came from and was all about why he left during the potato famine.

Then there was the tour of the castle and the 'authentic' dinner, which really does need to be in quotes. It was fun and campy. There was a kind of show during dinner too. Remember when we were driving along the highway, (at last, a highway, even if it was only for a few miles), and we saw the turrets of castles dotting the landscape in between suburbia?

Of course there were ancient cemeteries, at least ancient to Americans, and more coastal towns and so much seafood and so much walking and it was all wonderful.

We went with a plan in mind and stayed open, happily ditching plans whenever something better came along. It's still one of my favorite trips I've ever taken. I hope someday we can take another one. Maybe to New Zealand this time and a certain hobbit home. Love you. Love, Mom. More adventures to follow.

AUTHOR NOTES - MICHAEL ANDERLE

WRITTEN JANUARY 23, 2024

Thanks for sticking around for the post-story chat in these author notes because, let's face it – the books are over, and you could have just closed it down.

So, let's dive into something a bit off the beaten path today – the curious case of my memory, or rather, the lack thereof. (No thanks to Martha for setting off this thought process.)

The 'Forgettable' Benefit

In a life where memories are supposed to be the mental snapshots we treasure, my brain operates more like a live stream that doesn't save to the cloud.

Hell, it saves to nothing, as far as I can tell.

I've got this Teflon-like skill where past tragedies and epic fails just slide right off. Handy, right? I mean, who needs to hold onto past embarrassments when the brain gives you a shiny "Nope, don't remember" card every time? Now, it doesn't help very much when my wife starts with, 'Honey, did you remember…' because I know that the end of this discussion is going to suck a big bag of … carrots.

Memory's Top 5? More Like Top None

If you were to ask me about my most epic vacation, I'd draw a blank. Not because I haven't *been* anywhere note-worthy (if been all over the world), but because my memory bank seems to have a worse retention policy than a sieve. My top five trips? Ha! I'd be lucky to give you a top one, and even then, it's probably just the latest place I've been, because it's the only one I haven't managed to forget —yet.

I can't even remember which trip was Singapore and which was ...fuck... What was that city in Thailand? SEE!?

Imagination Over Memory

Now, don't get me wrong. While my rearview mirror might be a bit smudged (meaning, cracked the f#@# up) my windshield is crystal clear. I can dream up realms and plots like nobody's business, churning out tales across genres like a literary machine on crack coke (the drink, not the white stuff). It's almost as if life played a bit of give-and-take with my faculties—swapping out memory for a wild imagination.

Why the Forgetfulness?

Is this forgetful trait something etched into my DNA, or just a quirk of my character? Who knows? I can't remember if I ever knew enough to care except now that I'm getting older. So, I'm slapping a big ol' label on this experience called "life," dubbing it the best trip I've ever taken. I'm cruising through the prime of life without a care for the supposed "good old days" of high school heroics or college romances that, let's face it, *never happened*.

And by 'never happened,' I'm being brutally honest. That stuff that was wonderful for others? Yeah, it didn't happen for me. High school sucked @#R@ and college, while better than high school, was also a letdown (for me).

Perhaps that is more my fault because I barely came out of my personality shell, but it is what it was, and it wasn't great.

Yet, There's a Longing...

But here's the kicker—I sometimes wish I could just kick back and replay the greatest hits of my life.

Enter the tech stuff, like that fancy new Apple Vision Pro I've got on preorder. They say it's packing some serious 3D video magic, and I'm intrigued. Maybe, just maybe, it could be the external hard drive my brain's been missing.

When I receive this device, I plan to thoroughly test its features to see if it can effectively capture and store my memories in a clear and lasting way. If it works as I hope, I'll be able to keep a more permanent record of my experiences, beyond the fleeting and often unclear impressions that currently make up my recollections and report back. Could be I'll finally have a way to capture memories in more than just fleeting feelings and impressions.

The Takeaway

So, as we wrap up this session of author note musings, I leave you with this: I might not have a vault of vibrant vacation vignettes to share, but I've got a life journey that's second to none. Here's to steering our narratives toward a finale filled with joy, even if we can't recall every twist and turn along the way. And who knows? With a little help from our friend technology, maybe those memories will stick around for the encore.

Catch you in the next story, or if my memory allows, maybe sooner.

Ad Aeternitatem,
Michael Anderle

P.S. For those of you eager to follow my tech-laden odyssey or simply share in my excitement (and maybe even my neck pain), join the conversation and subscribe to my newsletter here: https://michael.beehiiv.com/

BOOKS BY MARTHA CARR

Other Series in the Oriceran Universe:

JOIN THE ORICERAN UNIVERSE FAN GROUP ON FACEBOOK!

CONNECT WITH THE AUTHORS

Martha Carr Social

Website: http://www.marthacarr.com

Facebook: https://www.facebook.com/groups/
MarthaCarrFans/

Michael Anderle Social

Website: http://lmbpn.com

Email List: https://michael.beehiiv.com/

https://www.facebook.com/LMBPNPublishing

https://twitter.com/MichaelAnderle

https://www.instagram.com/lmbpn_publishing/

https://www.bookbub.com/authors/michael-anderle